Death by Numbers

C. B. Burdette

Flower Child Publishing

Cover Design by James, GoOnWrite.com
Formatting by Polgarus Studio, polgarusstudio.com

ISBN-13: 978-0692025215
ISBN-10: 0692025219

To my best friend. You have fostered such creativity.

Thank you for putting up with me.

"Every man's life ends the same way. It is only the details of how he lived and how he died that distinguish one man from another."

-Ernest Hemingway

One

It was autumn in Georgia. The sun was still beaming down on the little town of Cherokee and most people were trying their best to soak up the last few warm rays of daylight before the crisp air of the night blew in. Dana Finkleton was just getting off work and coming home from work to relax at home with her family, when she drove through the local Chik-N-Dash.

She pulled through the drive-through and gave the mysterious voice on the other end her order. "I'd like to get one family bucket."

"Just one?" the voice on the other end asked.

"Just one," she said as she started to roll her manual window up.

Right as her window was coming to a close she could hear the cashier on the other side mention the total, "That's going to be $10.61, at the first window."

The Finkleton's were always strapped for cash. So much to the point where in her early forties, in 2010 Dana

1

was still driving her old beater that her parents had given her as a college graduation gift. Of course back then wasn't considered a beater, but was a beautiful expensive present to show their gratitude for her hard work. Of course back then Dana wasn't a Finkleton but a Debrowski.

When Dana was in high school she was the captain of the cheer-leading team and her boyfriend Billy Finkleton was the captain of the football team. They were high school royalty. Everyone and their mom knew of the couple's existence, even if Dana and Billy had no clue about theirs. Dana and Billy went to separate colleges, of course on football and cheer-leading scholarships. The summer before college they made the decision that it would be in their best interest to hold their romance off until after college. At first they kept in touch with letters, but by the time Christmas had rolled around, the letters to each other tapered off and they began to live their own separate lives.

The summer after freshman year of college Dana and Billy ran into each other at a firework stand the weekend before the Fourth of July. On her way to shop for fireworks Dana and her friend Jennie had a few roadies. Slightly tipsy, Dana dropped a box of sparklers on the ground and when she went to pick it up, a good looking guy of twenty something went to pick up the sparklers for her. He smelled of the musk of summer paired with a cheap cologne, a fragrance that she'd grown to love among men.

They both touched hands as they bent down for the sparklers. Dana let out a giggle and looked up to the dreamy man behind the sunglasses, "Thank you," she said as he handed them to her.

"No problem, but then again, I'd always be there for my Dana," he said to her. Reading the confusion on her face, he removed the sunglasses. "Don't tell me you've gone off to college and 5 months of no letters has made you forget about me already?"

"Billy!" she shouted as she leaned in to his embrace. "I thought you looked familiar but I couldn't pin down why." She studied his newly ripped body and explained herself, "you've just changed a little is all."

"I may have changed, but you're still as gorgeous as ever. What are you doing on the 4th of July?"

"Not too sure, me and Jennie were going to sit by the lake and drink while playing with sparklers. We're useless when it comes to the big fireworks. We'd probably end up shooting our eyes out."

"Why don't you come over to my parent's lake house. They went to the beach for the fourth, so me and some guys are having a party."

"I'm not going to just ditch Jennie."

"Then don't, bring her too," Billy shot her a smile, "I, ah, gotta pay for these and head out." He waved goodbye and drove off.

Dana brought her gal-pal to the party, but that didn't stop her from making sure that all of her time was spent with Billy. By the time everyone had gotten past the fourth drinking game, Billy and Dana were sneaking off to a wooded area by the lake.

"You realize how much I've missed you, right?" asked Billy.

"If you really missed me then why did you stop writing?"

"Our letters were already fizzling out. I was getting preoccupied with classes. You know how it goes, you were too. It doesn't matter why this or why that. What does matter is the fact that we're here now."

In that wooded area by the lake in North Georgia, Dana let Billy have his way with her. In Dana's mind, they had finally rekindled their love for one another. She thought the love they shared had never really left either one of their minds. They were just now able to act on their impulses. Nine months later Dana gave birth to her little impulse.

Billy and Dana got married a few months before their baby was born. After the first semester of sophomore year was over Dana and Billy moved back to the town they were from.. Going to college in 6 states away from one another would be too difficult when raising a family. Billy and Dana got married a few months before their baby was born. They believed that they were supposed to be a family at some point anyway, so they decided to go ahead and jump the gun. They said that they would enroll back in college once they were back on their feet and had a little nest egg stored in the bank so they wouldn't have to worry about the costs of living. Of course having a nine to five job is difficult enough on it's own, but with the addition of a newborn baby, they would never find time to go back to school. It would prove especially difficult to go back to school after years went by and they made more additions to their family.

By the time Dana arrived home it was seven at night. Leah, her oldest daughter had gotten a scholarship at a local university and didn't live at home anymore. One less child to have to pay for. Tony and Danny were both in high school and had just gotten home from football practice. Following in their father's footsteps they were always hungry. Feeding four mouths, three of which were like throwing food into black holes, proves difficult on factory wages.

Dana and Billy had gotten jobs working at local factories shortly after the birth of their daughter. Although the city they live in didn't have much going for it, it did have the factories. Given the economic status of the country, there wasn't any telling in how much longer they'd actually be able to even rely on their factory jobs. Lay offs were taking place at both of their companies and it was only a matter of time before either, or both of them, were laid off.

Dana placed the bucket of chicken in the middle of the table and laid out the plates and cups for her family to make their own plate when they got to the table. She filled up everyone's glasses with sweet tea and made sure that they had ice filling the cups to the brim. All of the boys came to sit around the table and Dana joined in the feast with them.

"How was work?" asked Billy. It was always the same opening question every single night. It always was followed with the same dull answer every night.

"Work was fine," said Dana. She shifted in her seat and continued, "Ten more workers in my division of the company got laid off."

"They must be keeping the best, and loosing the rest," said Billy, trying his best to cheer up his bride. Despite his balding, his physique hadn't changed as drastically as most middle-aged men.

Dana always would often reminisce about the past that she shared with Billy. She would constantly remind herself that she wouldn't change a thing. Whether it was the truth, or her trying to convince herself into happiness for the life she settled for, she would always enjoy moments like these. The ones where she would be sitting around the dinner table with her family, and realize that it wasn't always how much money was in the bank, but how much love was in the heart.

"What about you?" she asked Billy.

"Work was fine. Nothing too much going on, same thing different day."

The night rounded off the same way every day. Billy would read his football magazines in the bathroom, disposing the dinner that he'd indulged in hours earlier in the evening. Dana would wrap up the night laying in bed reading her novellas until she drifted off to sleep in deep dream where she would be able to fly away to a land where she would become something more than worker 109 in a factory line.

The next morning she rose up out of bed and threw her clothes on. Down to the kitchen she went, in search of food she could put in her sons' bellies before she shipped them off to school for the day. Upon opening the fridge she found butter and various jams. Some of her fondest memories from childhood were built on the foundation of toast. She took her time popping the toast into the toaster and when all eight pieces were done, she stacked them high on a plate and cut them diagonally in half. More pieces, makes it seem like there's more toast. She created a spread on the table and put the jam jars on opposing sides of the butter container. Right in front of them she laid out the toast.

Twenty minutes from then the alarms were going off around the house and she could hear the men in her life scurrying around to make sure they had everything put together on their backs and in their book-bags before making their way downstairs. Dana had made it a point that a family should try their hardest to make it to meals with one another, especially breakfast since it's the one that can start the day off right.

After ten minutes of meat-head sons shoveling food down their throat, they were ready and running to fly off to the bus stop. Dana picked up the breakfast remnants that were laying around the table, as Billy kissed her on the cheek and scampered out the door. She always wondered why it was that she was always the one stuck to cleaning the table. Not only did she take the time to prepare the meal, but she would always end up being the one to clean up after it as well. She didn't mind it too much, but it was one of a many on her list of pet peeves from around the house.

Her travel time to work was a grand total of fifteen minutes. Those fifteen minutes weren't from point A to point B, but they included her leaving her front door step, to clocking in and making her way to her station on the long row of seats in her line at the factory. She lived only six miles from the factory, which made it easier on her to do breakfast for her family on a daily basis. She had managed to get a job working at the cereal factory through one of her mom's friends who had worked for the company so long that she was able to retire. The friend had a special liking for Dana and made sure that by the time the kids were at the age where they could go to day care, she would have a job. Of course, factory jobs always have fairly decent pay, but just not the pay that her parent's had as she was growing up. Dana was an only child, so it meant that her parents could spend three times as much money on her as she could spend on her children.

She and Billy were only five years away from being able to retire from their jobs. They'd both put in twenty years, and both of the companies they each worked for had a retirement plan in place for it's workers where they could retire after twenty five years of work. Though they were always frugal when it came to money, once the kids left the nest and they'd retired from the factory they could live life more on a day to day basis, rather than paycheck to paycheck.

As she rolled in to work she saw a few of her coworkers taking boxes to their cars. 'Another day, another job lost' had become the motto of the factory. She parked in one of the parking spots beside her friends car and went over to give her condolences.

She walked up to one of her friends and reached around their shoulders and comforted her, "Jeez Sharon, I'm so sorry."

Tears streaming down her face, Sharon responded, "I really didn't think I would have been one of the ones laid off. I've been there longer than most of the managers combined."

"I know," said Dana, "They get all of these guys from the universities to come in and manage the company and all they do is stir the economic pot."

"If the factory was smarter about the wages around here, they'd promote the employees already working for them, instead of hiring on these big guys who demand three times the paycheck to be a manager than any of us would if we were promoted."

"I guess that's the benefit of having a college degree," Dana said as she tucked her friend's hair back behind her ear. "You can demand all you want, and get it if you have the diploma to back you up." She looked at her watch and realized what time it was, and that she needed to be inside before she was late. "I have to go, but give me a call. I'm going to miss you so much." She hugged her friend and went inside her work

As she walked through the doors she noticed that a lot of the people leaving with boxes weren't just her coworkers, but the coworkers that were stationed in the same area she worked in. Hopeful thinking started coursing through her brain. Could it be that she was one of the only ones that were kept to work in that area of the factory? It was possible, she thought, that maybe some of the cutbacks in the factory were being made overall as a whole, and that they were laying off people across the board in different areas, rather than just cutting off a whole production line.

She walked to the locker room inside of the factory where she worked for twenty years. Many of the lockers were donned with the infamous pink slip taped to the locker. As she rounded the corner, she could only hope that she would be one of the few in her station of the factory that didn't get let go. She walked up to her locker and put her palm up to the cold surface and let it cross the ridges of the locker door, as her hand slid over the pink slip that was indeed taped to her own locker.

With tears streaming down her face, far too similar to the tears she'd just brushed off of her friends face not even five minutes ago, she tried to control the anger that burned furiously inside of her. Twenty years she spent in this factory. Twenty years, 48 weeks a year, five days a week, ten hours a day, pinned up inside of this hell hole. She had even lost the ability to smell the fragrance of cereal wafting up out of a freshly opened box, because of all the time she spent around it here. Fuming, she stormed off to the company managers office in the middle of the factory. All of her coworkers stared her down as she banged her fists against the metal door that led into the office of the factory manager. It's hard to say whether or not they were staring at Dana because of how enraged she was, or because they too were enraged, but lacked the courage to do anything about it.

The door opened, and a white collar man in his thirties opened the door, "Mrs. Finkleton, what's going on?"

"Oh, I'm sure you know what's going on. Look at this pink slip in my hand," she gestured to the man, "Can you really not see what's going on."

"Dana, please. Come in my office, we'll talk."

"Oh, so now it's Dana!"

Looking around at all the bystanders Mr. Jones nodded to them and gestured his hand towards his office for me to step inside.

"Have a seat, I insist."

"This isn't much of a sitting matter, Mr. Jones."

"Mrs. Finkleton, you know as well as I do, that there are people all across the country having to deal with lay offs."

"I've worked here twenty years. Does that mean nothing to you or this corporation?"

He rested his head in his hands and looked up at her, "Dana, there are many people who have worked for factories for thirty years and been laid off."

"I'm five years away from my retirement."

"Many of the other people in this company are as well. We don't sit around calculating the years towards retirement before we lay someone off. Sometimes we just have to look at the statistics and see what areas are making more money. The area of your factory is being shut down as a whole. Another factory for the company in Ohio is going to be producing that line of cereal now."

"Can't you send me to some other section of the factory? I mean, I'll do anything," Dana pleaded desperately.

"It's out of my hands at this point," he stared at the phone on his desk and pulled a thought out of the back of his mind. "I do, however, have a cousin who owns a nearby gas station. A few nights ago he was mentioning that they were looking for an extra hand to work the cash register a few nights a week."

"Your advice for me losing my job of twenty years, is to go get a part time job as a cashier at a gas station?"

"It's really the best that I could do."

Dana stood up and headed towards the door, "Thanks, but I have a family to feed. I don't think a part time job will be much help."

"Well," said Mr. Jones, "The offer stands until they find someone. I always have a phone near me, just give me a call if you change your mind and want me to reach out to my cousin for you."

Dana waltzed out of the door and with great stride quickly picked up her items from the locker room and left the building. As she put her personals into the car, thoughts started spiraling into her head. What was she going to do? Her husband worked at a factory across town that manufactured cars, but he made the same wage that she did. One spouse paying the way for a family for four and working a job that wasn't even salary was going to be difficult in this economy. She even wondered how her husband would take the news. Every day at dinner when they'd talk about who had gotten laid off he would always mention, 'Well, I guess they're just keeping the best of the best', to keep her spirits high. Now that she too had been laid off, what would be said around the dinner table?

She had the whole day to kill, so she drove around. Living in North Georgia had the perks of scenic highways at only a short distance away. As her musty old beater creeped up the scenic route through the foothills of Georgia she fell into arms of nostalgia. Twenty years ago, she hadn't a worry in the world about money or the bills. What had happened to the life of that long-ago cheerleader? She had been deemed the most beautiful girl in school by the other students, and had planned on being the most successful girl as well. She had it all, beauty and the brains. All it took was one night to lead her down a path of twenty years hell and hardship.

The day was spent driving, not just the physical driving, but also the driving away of any unwelcome thoughts. Maybe she should just keep driving and never look back. Her daughter was already on a full ride for college, and her two sons were both in their last two years of high school and they'd be out the door and off to college themselves within a matter of three years at most. Billy could easily find another companion somewhere else. He would be the only bread winner anyway, what would it matter if she wasn't by his side? It would just be one less mouth for him to feed. What was even left back there? An old flame that was quickly burning that had forced her on a path of the repetitive waking up simply to go to work and come home to sleep.

Every day for the past twenty years had blended in with one another. She decided, that it would be best for her to go back and let the days continue to blend in. She did have a family after all. The ride back was more of a dragging back than anything. The constant anticipation of having to tell her family that she lost her job was eating at her mind. By the time she'd made it home it was five in the evening. She hadn't eaten anything since breakfast since her thoughts had jumped a time machine during her midday escape. Once she was inside she threw her purse on the couch and made her way to the kitchen to start dinner for her family. It was a spaghetti kind of night. When she was done cooking and had started setting the table her husband came through the door with their two sons.

"Honey, I'm home," he said cheerfully as he made his way in the door.

"Dinner's on the table if you guys wanna go ahead and have a seat," said Dana.

Once everyone was around the table Billy commented on the food, "I always tell the guys at work that my wife makes the best spaghetti." He slopped a huge fork load of spaghetti into his mouth, "John's wife is Italian and he always tries to size it up, but I have to stick a stern finger his way and say, 'Hell no'!"

"It's just out of a can, I'm sure John's wife's spaghetti is ten times better." Dana would usually play along with Billy, but tonight she wasn't in the mood to be swooned. Billy could tell that she wasn't acting her normal self. As could the boys.

"Mom, what's wrong? We love your spaghetti," said the blonde, while the one with the freckles and red hair shot glances between his parents.

"It's not the spaghetti, or how much you guys love it," she hesitated and continued, "I was laid off today at work."

Billy reached across the table to grab his wife's hand, "Dana, it's OK. We'll work things out." He looked to his sons and back to her, "I promise."

Later that night while she was laying in bed reading, she looked up and saw Billy standing in the doorway. "Hello, there." He walked further in the room and made his way to the bed. Sitting down on the bed he wiped his wife's hair back from her face and tucked it behind her ear. "Everything's going to work itself out."

"How are we going to prepare our boys for college on your income alone?"

"I didn't want to say anything earlier because I know your going through a rough time right now, but I got a promotion at work."

Gleaming she pushed the glasses up off of her face and onto the top of her head, "Why didn't you say anything at dinner? It would have lightened the mood a lot. How much of a raise?"

"Not too much, but now instead of making hourly wages, they're going to put me on salary. It could mean longer hours here and there, but they're going through the process of shifting everyone over to salary. It'll mean about four thousand extra dollars a year. It may not seem like a lot, since it'll be dispersed throughout the year, but it'll help."

"That's wonderful," she said. "Any bit helps."

"Maybe you could get a part-time job. We're getting older and I'd like to see you less stressed and around the house more."

"I'm not sure how I feel about a part-time job. It would definitely be a cut from what I had been doing."

Billy thought for a minute before saying, "Having no job at all would be an even greater loss."

"I suppose you're right." She stared at her husband and continued, "I threw a hissy-fit at work today when I found the pink slip."

He crawled under the covers with his wife and held her in his arms, "Oh yeah, tell me about it."

"Yeah, the other folks couldn't help but stare, so Mr. Jones pulled me into his office. You know, he mentioned one of his cousins owning a gas station in town and that they were actually looking for someone to work part time working the cashier."

"What did you say?"

"I basically threw my hands in the air and left, but he said that the opportunity would stay on the table until they had found someone to fill the spot."

"You should call him in the morning and find out more about it."

She fell asleep and in the morning she gave Mr. Jones a call and asked more about the job. Turned out that the cousin who owned the gas station was the husband of Dana's best friend in high school. When the cousin realized that it was 'the' Dana that his wife talked about non-stop, he couldn't help but hire her. Most would assume it odd that someone would hire, or even consider hiring someone over the phone. The owner of the gas station invited Dana to come in for a day. She would shadow one of the workers and would see if the job was the right fit for her.

The morning of her shadow day on the job, she made heart shaped pancakes for her family. Her explanation for them was that no matter what, she knew she would always have a home filled with loving people. The days leading up to the shadow, they did nothing but encourage her. The disappointment that she thought would've ensued from her job loss, turned out to be non-existent.

Pulling up in one of the parking slots beside the store she braved herself. She placed her sunglasses in the cup holder next to her and made sure her pressed button down shirt was tucked neatly into her khaki pants. She reapplied her lipstick, and smacked her lips together. She took a deep breath in and grabbed her purse and went inside the gas station. As she walked in, she noticed the only person in the store was a young clerk behind the check-out counter. "Hi, I'm here to do some job shadowing. Is Mr. Collins here?" she asked the girl.

"Oh! You must be my new coworker!" the peppy young blonde exclaimed, "I'll go get the boss-man for you."

When the blonde walked away, Dana couldn't help but think about how she was at the girls age. The girl couldn't have been over seventeen, and when Dana was that young, she shared the same spunk and joy for life as the young girl in front of her. Mr. Collins came out of one of the back rooms with the girl and introduced himself, "I'm so glad I finally get to meet you. My wife has told me all of the stories from yall's childhood."

"Oh, dear. I hope they weren't too damaging," said Dana.

"Not by any means. Now," he gestured to the young girl, "this is Claire, my youngest daughter. She helps out around the store when she's not at school. You'll shadow her, and she'll help show you the ropes and the in's and out's of the store."

Claire showed Dana the runs of the building. It almost took Dana for a surprise that she was actually shadowing a girl who wasn't even half of her own age. Having to shadow such a young girl brought back to life the reality of living on such a dead-end road.

The day drew to an end. It was around seven at night and Dana was used to being home with her family around this time. Mr. Collins had told her that she would only be working day shifts, but tonight would have to be an exception to the rule, just so she could learn what to do during the transitions of the daily duties.

Dana was straightening up some items on the shelf in front of the register when Claire asked her, "Hey Dana, would you mind looking over the register a minute?"

"Claire, I don't even really know how to work the thing."

"I just really have to go to the bathroom. It's pretty dead in here, I'll be quick, I promise."

"Well," hesitated Dana, "Sure, I don't see what harm it could do.

Dana came around to the opposite side of the counter and stood there so Claire could go to the bathroom. Right when Claire shut the door to the bathroom a customer walked in the door and went up to the counter.

"Oh, it's going to be just a second before I can help you," said Dana.

"I don't need any help," said the man. He pulled out a gun and put it in Dana's face, "Just open the register and put the money in one of your plastic bags and that'll be help enough."

Shaking and shocked, Dana continued, "But I don't have the code to the register, I'm just training."

"Are you fucking with me?" asked the man. "Put the damn money in the bag!" He waved the gun in her face.

"I seriously don't have the…" the gun went off. It took one bullet.

Two

Teddy Manchester had been a handful his whole life. From the time he was two until he was seventeen, he would create chaos for his parents. He had colic as a baby, the kind that forced his parents to put themselves on sleep shifts. When he did sleep it was usually during the day, when the parents were at work. Mrs. Manchester worked up until the day she gave birth, and didn't even take but a two week maternity leave from before she threw herself back into the whirlwind of her marketing business. Teddy's parents had work as their number one priority. Some of the family members will tell you that this was the reason he was a hell raiser. Raising hell to snag any nibble of attention that his parents would allow to fall off the table.

The Manchester family was one of the wealthiest and most highly respected families in Cherokee county of Georgia. Not only were Mrs. And Mr. Manchester well established in the marketing and advertisement community, but they also fell off of the tree of a long line of old money. Both of their parents ancestors were sharecroppers in Georgia and amazingly the money was well maintained and eventually invested. The company both families ended up investing in boomed, as did their pockets. It wasn't necessarily that the family needed to work for more money, it was just that their blood ran green. Where there was an opportunity to earn money, they would be found lurking in the shadows.

Most respectable families have beautiful children gleaming ear to ear, happy to simply be able to have their parents at beck and call for any of their wildest wishes and demands. Teddy, while beautiful, was one of the wildest children North Georgia had ever seen. At first his troubles started out with simply being disrespectful towards his parents. As he got older his transferred his attitude away from his parents and onto the teachers at his school. Teddy always struggled in school, but as he got older and progressed from basic math into the hands of algebra, his grades took an even deeper dive. Earlier in his life, his anger and outbreaks usually stemmed from the lack of attention his parents gave him. As he aged, it wasn't simply the lack of attention that was fueling the fire, but also his inability to comprehend certain mathematical skill. It seemed as though no matter how hard he studied, Teddy was bound to fail anything testing his skills.

In the eighth grade, one of his teachers expressed concern when it came to Teddy's grades. He looked into Teddy's files and even though he was never too bright of a shining star, he had never failed so many tests or assignments consecutively than he had during that semester. One evening after grading a midterm exam, his teacher gave his parents a call. When his mother picked up the teacher started, "Hi, I'm looking to speak to Mrs. Manchester."

"This is she. With whom am I speaking to? I'm sort of in a bind at the moment," said his mother.

"This is Mr. Stevenson from Glendell Middle School."

"I'm sorry, who?"

The teacher let out a deep sigh, and realized that maybe Teddy's parents were just as interested in his academics as Teddy was. "I'm you're son's math teacher."

"Ah, I see." She took her hand off of the mouse of the computer for a moment, and continued, "What sort of trouble has Teddy gotten himself into this time?"

"No sort of trouble. Not for now at least." He tapped his pen on his desk two times, "It's your son's grades that I'd like to talk to you about."

"He was slipping last year and in sixth grade as well, but I thought we'd gotten him back on track at the end of last year?"

"You may have, but I took a look at his records a day or so ago and I noticed that he'd never had so many consistent tests and homework assignments score failing grades. It looked as though his grades were more up and down in previous years, but this year it seems as though he's just not even bothering to put forth any effort. We do offer tutoring sessions at the school, if you're interested.

They have a scholarship program based on the family's income for it as well. It would allow him to study at a discounted rate if his grades were to improve."

"Money isn't an issue to us, Mr. Stevenson. As far as the studying goes, every night that I'm in town, he's studying in his room."

"If he is studying consistently, then maybe it's best to look into having him tested to find out if he has a learning disability."

"Do you really think that, that could be his issue? I mean he's always been a problem child. Could something like that come from having a learning disability as well?"

"I'm sure it's possible. If you talked to the guidance counselor she would be able to help you find someone to do the testing."

Mr. Stevenson got Mrs. Manchester in touch with the guidance counselor to help find a list of psychologists in the area. Once Mrs. Manchester had tracked down the most expensive, and well sought after one in the area, she made an appointment for her son. Little did she know, that on the same day that her son would need to be taken for his appointment, she would have to fly out of town unexpectedly the day before for a meeting with a possible wealthy client. Mr. Manchester also had to fly out of town for the week. They both had meetings that could possibly bring in huge accounts for the companies they worked for. None of their friends had the day off either, so no one was able to take him to the appointment. With all the money that the family had, one would assume that they would've been able to pay someone to take him to his appointment. They had little time or energy to be devoted to their son, and once again Teddy had to deal with being put on the back burner.

Teddy's junior year of high school was the most intense year that the family had ever seen. The passing of two grandparents, meant that his own parents would have to be primarily in town focusing on how to deal with the estates of their parents. Death not only brings up financial responsibilities, but emotional ones as well. If someone doesn't understand how to deal with these emotional circumstances, they might end up on a downward spiral. Luckily for Teddy this didn't happen to his parents, but they did let their emotions stay so locked up within themselves that they gave even less to Teddy.

It was the week after fall vacation, which also meant it was the week after midterms at Gleaming Hights High School. Many of the students had made it a point to make sure that their grades were steadily on high, simply because if it altered their GPA, it would alter how a contending college would view the future student. Teddy had decided that no matter how difficult it was going to be to get his grades up, he was going to give it his all. He stayed up two nights in a row with some of his best friends studying math. It was really the only class that gave him issues. He excelled in anything artistic and was beyond capable in English and Geography.

As the teacher made her way down the aisles with midterms in her hand, Teddy began to sweat profusely.

The teacher laid down the tests on the desk with the back facing upwards, so no neighboring desks would be able to see the score of the person sitting next to them. Teddy also had to wonder if this was also a way for the teacher to have to avoid that awkward moment, when a teacher lays an 'F' on a desk, and a student catches their eye. Finally, she had made it back to his desk. Teddy always sat at the back of the classroom. He didn't sit there by choice in this one, however, she had created a seating chart at the beginning of the year. Either by luck, or just assumption, she had determined that this seat in the back corner of the classroom would be the right place for him to sit. She passed his desk and laid the test flat in front of him. It took him a good five minutes before he flipped it over. 'F'.

"You have got to be kidding me!" He shouted as he stood up from his seat. "I studied for days on end for this test," he looked around the classroom at all of the students staring back at him, as well as his teacher who was in complete shock, "How in the hell can I get an 'F' after studying for two days?"

"You didn't get the answer's right, Teddy," said his teacher looking on, feeling the overwhelming sadness that Teddy was putting off.

"This is bullshit, you're bullshit!" he said towards his teacher.

"Get out of my classroom, Mr. Manchester. Go to the office now."

He threw his hands up in the air and shouted, "I didn't do anything!"

The teacher, furious, pointed towards the door, "OUT!"

On his way down the hall he ripped up his test and threw it in the air. Once he'd gotten to the principles office he sat down in the line of students who were ahead of him. A friend of his was sitting a few chairs down. He leaned forward to start talking to him, "What're you in for?"

"I threw a paper airplane across the class and it hit a girl in the eye," he said as he laughed to himself. "What about you?"

"Remember that math midterm I studied with you and the guys for, for two days straight? Well, I got an 'F' on it and started shouting."

"Dude you gotta be kidding, you studied so hard. There has to be some kind of accomplishment for that alone. Like fifty bonus points or something."

The office clerk behind the desk shushed the two, "Shh! No talking. You are all in trouble as it is, there's nothing you should be willing to talk about here."

He watched a few kids go in and out of the office. By the time his buddy came out he was half way to falling asleep.

"Good luck bro-ski," said his friend.

"Thanks, I'm going to probably need it."

The principle came out and shouted, "Teddy Manchester. In my office, this instant."

As he went into the office he could feel the steam coming out of the principles ears. It had been a long hard ride for Teddy. He was no stranger to the principle's office, and he knew all of the office clerk by name.

"So," started the principle, "what makes you think you have the right to talk to a teacher the way you did."

"I really don't know," said Teddy.

"Well, how about we start with this. Why do you think you should have the ability to put your low grades off on a teacher? Why can't you accept responsibility for your actions. If you don't study, you reap what you sew."

"That's the thing though, I did study. I studied my ass off. Two days straight, near all nighters both time."

"Maybe you should consider studying as you're taught things, rather than trying to cram two nights before. Things have a tendency of lasting longer in long term memory, than they do in the short term." The principle stared down at his palms and looked up at the student, "I'm going to have to do something about your actions today."

"I didn't do anything though," Teddy said as he began to get anxious, "No one got hurt, I just stated the facts. It was total crap that I studied so long and it did me no good. I swear it's like that woman is out to get me. I can never catch a break."

"Teddy, you can't talk about your teacher like that. Not only is it disrespectful, but it also puts the notion that it's OK to speak rudely to teachers in the minds of other students. I just can't have that at my school."

"So what are you going to do," Teddy asked as he crossed his arms.

"Sadly I'm going to have to use you as an example. You can't just talk to your teachers any way you choose. You can't stand up in the middle of their classroom and shout at them, just because you're unhappy with a grade you received. If everyone did that, the school system would go haywire. I'm going to have to suspend you for a day."

"Suspension? Why can't I just have detention? It could even be multiple days of detention, just please not suspension."

"There are serious consequences to serious actions, Mr. Manchester. I will notify your parents this afternoon about your upcoming absence from school."

"But you can't do this!"

"Excuse me, Mr. Manchester," The principle said angrily as he stood up from his desk, "You need to leave my office and go to your next class, before I add more days to your suspension."

As he walked through the halls he realized that he had forgotten to get a tardy pass from the office, to show that he wasn't actually tardy, but had been sitting in the principle's office. Just as he was about to turn around and walk back, he decided that he wasn't going to go to the principles office after all. Instead of having to go back and get a slip to enter a classroom, he was just going to ditch the rest of the day. When he turned a corner he found his ex girlfriend standing at her locker.

"Hey pretty lady," he said as he leaned up against the locker next to hers.

Ashley rolled her eyes and looked at him, "What do you want Teddy?"

"Just wanted to say hey to my favorite girl."

"If I'm you're favorite girl then why were you seen kissing some random girl from another school at a party last week?"

"I was drunk," he shrugged, "someone brought beer, I'd had a few and she was blonde so she made me think of you, so I couldn't help myself."

"You must have lost your mind. Do you really think that's going to make me interested in you again?"

"I'm sorry, OK. I just miss you, and I'm awkward and just being around you throws me off. I never know what to say around you, and when I think I do, it only takes a few minutes before I realize I don't."

"Coming from you," she said as she leaned her books into her chest, "that means a lot."

"What class are you about to go to?" Teddy asked her.

"Depends, where were you headed?"

As he wrapped his arm around her shoulder he said, "I was thinking you should come with me for a little lesson in romance."

They walked leisurely out of the schools side door and off to the bus ramp. They kept walking until they got to a nearby wooded area that wasn't too far from the school. This was one of the main places that everyone would go when they ditched. It was amazing that none of the faculty had caught on. The wooded area between the school and a gas station at the end of the road was the perfect place for kids to ditch. They didn't have to go too far to get back to their next class, and if they wanted to kill the whole day here, it was still close enough for them to be able to get back on a bus without their parents even knowing.

Once they had gotten deep enough in the woods for them not to be seen through the trees, they put their things down. They started talking about things that they had done lately. Since they had only stopped talking to one another a week ago, there wasn't too much that they needed to be caught up on. After they reconnected, they began to rekindle their lust for one another.

When their make out session had reached thirty minutes, Ashley pulled away from Teddy's embrace, "I have to go."

"Why? We were just getting started. I missed you," said Teddy as he hoped he could convince her to stay with him.

"I already missed one class, I don't want to miss another one."

"But what's skipping one more class really going to do?"

She reapplied her lip-gloss and stared back at her teenage dreamboat, "Look, I'm having a party tonight at my house. You should be there."

"Sounds good. I wont miss it."

"Better not," she said, just before she planted one more kiss on him before running off back to school.

After she left, he exited the woods and went to get in his car in the parking lot. He decided that he was just going to go home, to hell with school. On his way home Ashley sent him a text message. It read, 'Party starts @ 10!'. Just as he looked down at his phone, he heard a loud honking noise. He looked up and jerked his car back into his lane. With his focus shifted onto the cell phone, he'd let his car get into the passer lane while someone was already driving in it.

He stopped at a coffee shop on his way home. At least if he was going to leave school, he wouldn't have to go straight home. When he went in, he took his headphones and laptop with him. There he would be able to play video games online and kill time before getting home. He wasn't sure whether or not his parents would be home before him, so he tried to time it so that he was able to walk through the door around the same time he would any other day.

When he finally made it home around four thirty, he unbuckled and let out a deep breath. There was no way that his parents would be able to find out about him skipping school. They would definitely know about him being suspended tomorrow, though. He put his laptop back into his book-bag and walked into the front door.

"What the hell is wrong with you, boy?" exclaimed Mr. Manchester.

"I don't know, sir," replied Teddy.

"Look over there at your mom," his dad gestured with his hands towards where his mom was sitting in a corner of the room with tears rolling down her face. "Look at how you've made her feel. Is that fair?"

"I'm sorry, but it also wasn't fair that I studied for two days, nonstop and I still couldn't pass the math midterm."

"It's not just about the grade, Teddy." His mom stood up from where she was standing and moved forward, "It's also about the way you handled yourself when you found out about the grade. You shouted at your teacher. It's not her fault that you didn't pass the test."

"Not only did you yell at your teacher, son," he dad jumped in, "but you also yelled at your principle. Low and behold we get a call earlier this afternoon about you being suspended over something so miniscule, that you could've dealt with emotionally. On top off that, two hours later we get a phone call saying that you didn't even go to the rest of your classes after you went to the office."

"I would've had to go back to the principle's office to get a tardy slip," he tried to justify, "I didn't want to have to face the office clerk and the principle again after all the drama."

"So you thought it would be a better idea to skip all together?" asked his mom. When her son didn't give her an answer, a thought pinged in her head. "Where were you even at during that time?"

"I was at the coffee house," Teddy told her. He thought that it'd be best for him to leave out the part about him making out with Ashley. That would just make the whole he was digging even deeper. "I was trying to kill time so that I could get here at the same time I always do, so that you guys wouldn't know that I skipped school."

"Did you really think that, that would work?" asked his dad.

"You guys never seem pay me much attention anyways, I didn't think you'd find out about me skipping school."

"Well, guess what? We did, and we're furious. I know your laptop is in your bag, as are your keys," said his dad.

"So what?" Teddy asked.

"So hand them over, you're on restriction until further notice."

"But…"

"But nothing. Now!"

Teddy handed over his keys and made his way upstairs to his room. Around eight that evening his mom brought dinner up to him. She left the food there without saying anything. Around nine he got a text from Ashley, 'U better b here tnight', it said. He had almost forgotten about the party. He knew that he would be able to go if he waited for his parents to go to sleep. They were on the road so much that when they actually were home, they would hit the hay as early as possible to catch up on sleep.

On his way to the stairwell he passed his parent's bedroom. He could hear the TV. running and since all of the house lights were off, it would mean that they were either barely awake or they had already fallen asleep. He crept down the stairs and made his way to the kitchen. Once he was in the kitchen he looked on the counter-top and found his keys inside of his mom's purse. Going through his mom's purse alone made him feel guilty. Add to that the guilt that he was about to sneak out on top of giving his parents such a rough day, just added to it.

Once he was in his car, he made his way over to Ashley's house party. Halfway there he realized that he was running low on gas. "Damn-it, I thought I had half a tank when I left the house," he mumbled to himself. Hopeful that he wouldn't see anyone his parents knew, he pulled over to the next gas station he saw and got out to pump gas. He only had cash on him so he went into the store the pay the attendant.

He'd heard about this gas station getting robbed a few weeks ago. It was plastered all over the news, 'Lady killed by robber on the first day of work', read the headlines. A robbery is bound to happen at a gas station at least once in the duration of the store being opened. Plus, what were the odds that it would happen again where the odds that it would happen again, just as he was there. Far too slim, he thought.

When he walked through the doors and up to the cashier, he noticed how cute she was. "Man, it's a good thing you weren't here when the gun went off," said Teddy, with his ever so charming way with words.

The girl stared at him, "I was training the woman who got shot. I had to go to the bathroom, so she stood in for me at the register. It should've been me that got shot."

"Wow, I'm so sorry. I had no clue."

"It's no big deal, you didn't know, after all. What pump are you at?"

"Pump two, just put twenty dollars on it, please."

"Sure thing. Be safe out there, you don't even look old enough to be driving this late."

"How old do I look?" asked Teddy.

"Old enough to know when a girl isn't interested," said the store owner as he came out from the back of the store.

"I'm sorry sir," Teddy said confused.

"That's my dad," she said with a smirk.

"Yes, I am her dad, and I think you should be heading home Mr. Manchester."

"Oh, how do you know who I am?" Teddy asked, puzzled.

"It's a small town, everyone knows everyone. Be safe out there."

"Will do, sir."

Teddy paid the cashier and pumped the gas outside in his car. Every emotion was trickling through his body. He didn't know why, but he knew that this was the line. The line had been drawn between troubled teen, and horrible son. It would've been one thing to have embarrassed his parents with his failing grades, but to add on top of that the mistreatment of his teachers and those looking out for him really would have done him in. His parent's were at their wits end with him, and he knew that he was going to have to do something to change it. Tomorrow he would start fresh. He would go to the party tonight, just to hang out with Ashley for a little while, but then he would head home. The thought of even having a drink had completely evaded him. It donned on him what a crappy son he'd been for leaving the house after everything that he'd put his parents through earlier in the day.

When he was done pumping the gas he put the nozzle back on it's holster, hopped in the car, and he put his seat belt on. He reached for his phone to text Ashley that he'd be on his way over to her house in just a few minutes. Placing the phone in his passengers seat, he adjusted his own chair. He started the car and drove out of the gas station parking lot and came up to an intersection when his phone went off. Teddy reached down to grab his phone.

Just then he heard the two loud semi's honking their horns. By the time he looked up it was too late. Two semi's were passing through the intersection at full speed. His car came across the intersection at the exact time when the two trucks were about to pass each other. Instead of simply passing each other, they each took halves of Teddy's car. It took two semi's.

Three

Frank Thomas grew up in Mississippi, with four brothers and three sisters. His mom worked a third shift at the local textile factory and his dad was a not so handy handyman. With his mom working the third shift, it meant that she would be able to stay at home with the youngest kids and to be able to see the older kids off to school. His dad would work during the day and would spend the night home with the family.

The house he grew up in wasn't in one of the largest houses around town. There were only three bedrooms to house ten people. It also wasn't in one of the nicest neighborhoods around either. However, being in the middle of Mississippi, where the majority of people lived in the boonies, it didn't really matter what side of town you lived on because nearly everyone was secluded anyway. Frank and his four brothers shared a room, and the girls shared their own room. There were two sets of bunk beds and one twin bed in his room, and two bunk beds and a twin bed in the girls room.

Mrs. Thomas gave birth to Frank when she was only 19. Even though this would seem young to start a family, she already had given birth to a son and daughter prior to having Frank. Fortunately for him, this would mean that he wouldn't be the one under the pressure to help take care of the family. Don't get the situation wrong, Mr. and Mrs. Thomas took good care of their children, but taking care of 8 kids can call for extra hands. They always laid the responsibility of the younger children on the older two. It was always up to them to have the most difficult of chores, like mopping the floor, or worse helping change the diapers of the babies.

Frank was young enough amongst the children so that he wouldn't have to do some of the stringent things his older siblings had to do, however he was still old enough to be considered one of the men of the household. He would always be the son that the dad would ask to join for many 'manly' adventures. Frank was the son that he would take into the woods to hunt deer. He was also the son that he would take with him just about anywhere he could take him, so he could show off his son. It wasn't necessarily that Mr. Thomas favoritized his second eldest son, it was just that he was the one he had more of a bond with. Frank was the one who pitched less fits, and was never too difficult of a child to be around.

When Frank was only 14 years old his father was killed while doing a service call. He was a jack of all trades, which basically meant that he knew a little about a lot. Rather than specializing in plumbing, or carpentry, or painting, he could do a little bit of it all. One afternoon he was called to work by an older lady across town. She needed some help cleaning out her gutters, and when he was about to climb down the ladder, it gave way underneath his weight and came crashing to the ground. He had fallen two stories, and ended up breaking his neck in the fall.

After the death of his beloved father, Frank couldn't handle the pressure that the family was under. His dad made the majority of the money, and while his mom's job gave her a decent paycheck, it still wouldn't be near enough to make all of the ends meet for a family of nine. Franks older brother and sister picked up part time jobs after school at the local grocery store as baggers. Though it wasn't much, it was a good supplement for the family to have. With the older kids gone during a good portion of the afternoon, the weight of chores and family duties fell on the shoulders of Frank. Already having to deal with the intensity of losing his father, the burden of having to take care of his younger siblings was too much.

One day in the middle of the night Frank slipped out of the door of his bedroom with just a few items in a back and he hit the road. He knew that his family needed him now more than ever, but he knew he would never be able to fill the shoes of his older brother around the house, more less the shoes of his father. There wasn't any plan given to where he would go, or what he would do when he got there. It was just the simple notion that he knew he had to escape.

When he finally stopped walking he was in a little town about forty minutes away from his family. He scrambled for what little change he had in his pocket and used it to buy a hot dog from the little restaurant kiosk within the gas station. There was a small booth sitting against a window in the back corner of the gas station. Frank sat down in it, despite the fact that it was right beside the men's bathroom, and nauseating vapors were emanating from it. About five minutes after Frank sat down to eat, a middle aged man came out of the bathroom.

"Kind of late for a guy your age to be out, isn't it?" asked the man.

"I guess." He hesitated a moment and thought about the prospects of whether or not this man could actually take him further away from home. He realized that no adult man would help a child run away, but he might help a runaway return home. "I ran away from home a few days ago and was trying to get back to my family."

The man sat on the opposite side of the booth from him, "Not so easy being a boy on his own, is it?"

"No sir, I guess not."

"Well where ya headed? Maybe I could help you get back."

"My family's from Louisiana."

"Damn, you sure did travel far. What part?"

"A small town just outside of the city limits of New Orleans."

"You don't sound creole?" the man asked suspiciously.

"I'm not. My parents were Louisianans by way of Alabama."

"Ah, I see," said the man with skepticism. "Well, listen here, I have a shipment that I need to make and it just so happens that I have to go to New Orleans to deliver it. How would you like for me to take you back home?"

Elated to get further away, Frank took up the offer that the man was handing him, "Of course. I would really appreciate it."

The two made their way through Louisiana and as they got closer to New Orleans the man spoke up, "You want me to stop at a pay phone so you can let your parents know that you're on the way home?"

Shocked and unsure of what to do, Frank just sat there.

It took him a little while to respond, but after a minute or two of silence the driver looked over at the boy, "You're not really from Louisiana are you?"

"No," said Frank as he stared at his hands.

"Damn-it. I should've known when you sounded straight out of the swamps of Mississippi." The driver could tell that he'd hurt the boy's feelings, "Look I'm sorry. I really don't know what to do. I would drop you off at the police station, but then they'd try to arrest me for abducting some kid. Why did you run away from home in the first place?"

"I have eight brothers and sisters."

"Well that's no reason to run away. What? Did you just not get enough attention from your parents, or something?"

"No, my dad gave me a lot of attention. But he died last month."

The trucker's chest sank as he was hit with what the boy had just told him. He gave heavy thought to just taking him back to where he came from, but then a reality sunk in. It would probably be less of a burden on the mom if she had one less mouth to feed. Yes it would take a heavy toll on the family emotionally, but after they'd moved on with their lives it would make the situation of having one income more spreadable amongst the family.

"Alright then. I have a proposition to make," said the trucker.

"What's that?" asked Frank.

"I'll take you on the road with me. If anyone asks, you're my son. You'll read books while we travel, and I'll make sure that you're learning about as much as possible. I'm not much of a teacher, but I can show you the road of life."

The trucker certainly did teach Frank how to use the reigns of life. Frank traveled with him for the next five years, until he turned nineteen. The trucker was getting more and more calls for business, so he began expanding his trucking company. One afternoon when he was pulling a load from Iowa back to Mississippi, he picked up a couple burgers from a fast food restaurant. Apparently he'd had too many burgers and ended up having a heart attack. Frank was like a son to him. He was even left in the will to take over the trucking company.

Losing two father figures in a matter of five years can take a toll on a young man. Especially one who also ran away from home and has no ties to his former family. He did however, now have his own trucking company. Even though he had many drivers working for him, he often took to the road himself. It was somewhat of a release for him. Traveling started to course through his veins and there was nothing like a good drive to get the upheavals of life out of his mind.

As he grew older he realized the difficulty of having a relationship while on the road. He went in and out of relationships. His love interests would always ask him to stay home. Why did he need to be out on the road when he had so many people working for him and bringing in the money on their own? He would always take the initiative to end the relationship there. Whenever a woman he saw interest in questioned his reasoning for driving, he knew that there was nothing there for him. He needed someone who could understand what life on the road meant. Sadly, there weren't too many woman who would understand what that lifestyle would entail. The ones that did were usually whores that would knock on truck doors in the middle of the night at truck stops.

Frank would often let these girls into his truck. The best part about the girls was the fact that they were always good for the moment, but never had any strings attached to them. He could just pick up in the morning and get on with his travel and not worry about calling some girl. Sometimes, especially on cold nights, the girls would be more scarce. These nights were the ones that he would have to get his socks knocked off to a girl in a video. The videos he watched were often the cheap ones he'd find in the truck stops. Those or the girls in magazines were just as good to him.

One day on one of his trips from Mississippi to Virginia, he got a phone call from his office clerk.

"Mr. Thomas," said the clerk, "There's been a crash with one of the company trucks, in Georgia."

"What happened?" asked Frank.

"The police are still investigating, but it happened in the middle of the night, and they believe that a young male was crossing an intersection when he didn't have a right away. He wasn't just hit by one of our semi's, but he was also hit from one coming in the other direction."

"Damn. I assume the boy didn't make it?"

"No, sir. Broke the car right in half. They need you in the town. Insurance companies and lawyers have already declared that neither of the semi's were over the speed limit, they were perfectly within the law. They've deemed it at the fault of the boys. The shipment that was in the truck needs to be reclaimed."

"I'll be passing through Georgia in the next four hours. Could you give me the information for the person of contact for me to reach when I get in town?"

"Sure thing," the clerk gave him the information, which Frank jotted down on the back of a napkin.

When Frank made it to the small town in Georgia where the wreck had occurred, he made his way to the towing station. Originally the police had taken the truck into custody, since they saw it as being some proof of evidence of what could've happened. When they found out that the trucks weren't at fault, and it was indeed the young boy who caused the wreck, they released the truck into the hands of a towing company. The load Frank was carrying to Virginia was a lighter load, and he could easily double up on the cargo trailer. He pulled into the towing station and realized that this could very well set him back a few hours. Since he'd been driving since the early hours of the morning he would have to come off of the road soon, which meant that it would be another day before he could get to Virginia. It was an easy process for him to get the cargo trailer from off the back of the truck and get it loaded and attached onto the back of his. As he was leaving the towing business, he asked the man how long he could keep the truck there. The man at the desk told him that the truck could stay their for one hundred and eighty days before they would gain the ownership of the vehicle. He thanked the man and told him that he'd have a representative come out and pick up the truck some time within the next two weeks.

Once he got back on the road, he noticed he had only a few hours he could drive before having to call it a night. He really needed to haul ass if he was going to make the shipment on time to Virginia. It was only responsible for him to go ahead and let his client know that there had been an issue and it was possibly going to take him longer than he originally planned.

Frank gave his client a call and when he told him about the accident he hardly gave any sign of empathy, "I understand that you're company has dealt with some issues in the past few days, but we really were planning on that shipment arriving here by tomorrow at noon," said the man.

"I'm driving as safely and quickly as possible to make sure that your shipment does arrive in time, however there is a chance that it could arrive later in the day than we originally expected. There was an unforeseen event that took place, and even though I wish I could say that I'll be there at noon, there is a chance that I wont be able to."

The man on the other line was upset, but knew there was nothing that either one could do about the situation. Fortunately after a death has occurred, people become more understanding about situations being out of anyone's control. Frank drove as far as he could that afternoon, but when eight o'clock rolled around he had to get off the road since he'd been traveling since six that morning.

When he finally stopped for the night he found himself in one of his favorite towns in North Carolina. Not only was the nature of North Carolina aesthetically pleasing, but so were it's women. Of course being on the road all of the time without anyone to come home to can make a man lonely. Certainly, there's no need for a man on the road to be lonely when he could easily buy the time of some young twenty something year old. He would be able to get all of the attention he ever wanted, just by throwing down a fifty dollar bill. Being the owner of a large trucking company, and being a trucker himself, with no family to pay the way for, meant that he could spend as much money as he wanted at these places. This also meant that all the girls at any given strip club he attended would remember him. Even if he only made his way through the state twice in 6 months, they would know him by name, just because of the fact that he would lay down more money in those two days, than most people would in a months worth of visits.

There was one club in particular that he loved in North Carolina. He would make sure that no matter what route he was taking, he would be sure that he passed by Cat's Meow. Although all of the girls there were some of the best looking girls in the state, there was one in particular that he was more fond of than any of the others. Her name was Candy and she was easily the smartest girl in the club. She was probably the smartest girl in the state. She started working at the club when she'd just got out of high school. Her dad was physically abusive and her mom didn't do anything about it except deny the fact that it was happening. She knew that it would've only been a matter of time before she was dead if she didn't leave the house.

What Candy also knew, that not so many of the other girls in the club knew, was that she wouldn't be able to work in a strip club her whole life. She had always gotten straight A's in high school, and she made a point that she would do the same in college. Though she had a scholarship to a nearby community college, she knew it would only pay until her bachelor's degree program was over. So, she worked five nights out of the week so that she would be able to save up for her graduate degree program without the worry of having to take out student loans which she'd end up repaying. The money that she made at the club also helped her to live on her own, outside of the abusive household that her mother had chosen for them.

Frank very possibly loved Candy. He had never had a real girlfriend growing up, given that he was on the road from age fourteen and was always around an old trucker. Even the women he had lust for in the past never had the substance to keep his interest. Whenever he was with Candy, even though he was paying for her time, he had more intellectual stimulation than he'd ever had with a woman. There were often times where he would just pay her to go to the private room to talk about life and ideals they both had. Of course, there were many times when he thoroughly enjoyed her assets.

He walked into the club and had a few drinks at the bar. Being primed up was a necessary thing for Frank. He was a great businessman, but being charming wasn't his forte until he had two drinks in him. Sitting at the bar he looked around for Candy and didn't see her anywhere.

When the bartender made her way back down to his seat, he asked her, "Is Candy working tonight?"

"Yeah," said the girl, "She's in a VIP room. She should be out in about ten minutes."

"Alright, thanks," said Frank. Just the simple thought of her being in the VIP room with some scumbag made his skin crawl. He knew that she was so much more than a body.

Finally when Candy was done, which felt like forever to Frank, she came out and walked up to the bar. "I thought I saw a familiar face," she said as she leaned over him. "Where you been? I've missed you."

"You know, driving," he said.

"Come with me," said Candy as she steered him towards one of the back rooms.

Once they were in the room Candy started kissing him. "As much as I really like this, I would much rather talk with you this time around. Just spending time with you is always a pleasure. I miss having someone to just talk to."

"I'm all ears," Candy said as she shifted into the seat beside him. "What's new?"

"Nothing really, just traveling from point 'A' to point 'B'. One of the trucks in my company ran into a car that pulled out in front of him so I had to pick up a load. Turns out that doing that it would mean me not making it to my point 'B' by the time they needed their shipment in."

"That's too bad," she said.

Frank could tell that Candy was out of her usual bubbly personality, "Everything O.K. with you?"

"Yeah, I'm fine," she said. She hesitated, then looked him dead in the eyes, "Actually it's not that fine. I'm having issues with some of the girls here. They've always been catty, but the past two months around here have been total hell."

"Why, what's happened?"

"I'm not sure, I've never been really good friends with any of the girls here, but now I just totally feel like I belong on misfit island with all of the other misfit toys. They've just been really bitchy lately."

Just then a heavy knocking came from the wall outside of the VIP room Candy and Frank were sharing. "Knock, knock," said a girl as she opened the curtain. She had a customer standing there with her.

Candy jumped up, "Kat! I'm in here with someone!"

"Well," said the girl as she and her customer closed the curtain behind them, "I can see that you're physically in here with someone, but I can also see that he has no interest in doing anything with you. Given the fact that I have this nice customer with me who actually would like to have a little fun, I think I'm going to go ahead and take priority of this room."

"Frank paid me to use the room," said Candy.

"He may've paid you to use it, but you obviously haven't used his money well. I mean, give the guy his money's worth. At least take your top off."

Frank took the opportunity to speak up, "Not everyone comes here to get in the pants of a prostitute that's trying to disguise herself as a stripper."

"Excuse me?" asked Kat.

"You heard me. Some people actually come to talk to the women here."

"That's the most idiotic thing I've ever heard."

Frank got closer to the girl, "Could it possibly be because you're an idiot, who no one would ever have an interest in actually getting to know?"

"Leave the girl alone!" shouted the man in the corner of the VIP room.

"Get out!" Frank said to the man.

"Gladly, but I'm bringing back management."

The man left and Frank asked the girl, "Are you the one going around giving Candy hell?"

"It's not just me, it's all of the girls. She pulls customers all of the time, making it hard as hell for any of us to make money. Therefore, we can't stand her."

"Think about it like this you little bitch, maybe the first girl anyone sees in this shit hole is Candy. Shes far better looking than anyone else here, and by the time they even pass two sentences between one another they can already tell that she has at least 100 IQ points on any of you."

Kat turned her attention away from Frank and focused on Candy. She lunged at the girl. Kat was 5'9 and all one hundred and fifty pounds of muscle, while Candy was 5'4 and barely ninety five pounds. Kat had a hold on Candy and Frank knew that she would end up severely hurt by the insane girl if he didn't do something. Frank went over to the girls and got Kat off of Candy. He pinned her down by the throat and held her there for three minutes, while shouting at her.

Finally the managers at the club made their way back to the room, but by the time they had it was too late. Frank had killed the bitchy stripper that was making Candy's life a living hell. It only took three minutes before she died of asphyxiation.

Four

Jenny Lanskie was the only daughter to Annie and Bo Lanskie. Both of the parents were younger, in terms of how old people are in the modern day when they have children. Even though the parents were barely in their twenties, they still gave Jenny everything her little heart desired. Bo worked as a manager at his fathers restaurant that his dad owned since the 60's. Their life's were basically handed to them on a silver platter because of how well off Jenny's grandparents were. Even the home that the couple moved in to after they got married was paid for by the parents.

A few summers after they got married, Bo's dad retired fully from the restaurant, giving room for Bo to take over the company. He took it over and ran it well, and had even more money for him and his wife to flaunt around. One night during their many escapades to somewhere luxurious, they conceived their daughter who would be born nine months later.

After Jenny was born, her mom decided that she would have her tubes tied. She had a condition that could possibly cause her to either miscarry any future children, or it would give her a heightened percentage of a chance that she'd have a child with birth defects. Annie and Bo were content with having one child to look after. In fact, they would much rather have one child running around than having multiple children with birth defects that they would have to tend to constantly. Little did they know that their decision to have a little girl who they would spoil, would mean that she would become one of the biggest gold diggers in the south.

Mr. and Mrs. Lanskie were able to give their daughter anything her heart could desire. Being able to, they definitely took advantage of it. They would hear horror stories at work about their friend's punishing their children and taking away all of their privileges. It would be appalling for them to think that some child should have to either earn right to play with his toys, or even have to earn the right to be bought toys. It wasn't necessarily that the parent's of Jenny had so much money to throw around, but the fact that they think all children should have the chance to have what their heart desires. People have only one childhood, and a kid shouldn't be robbed of his just because he may make a few mistakes here and there. That's what childhood is for.

One day when they took a trip to the circus Jenny had a huge meltdown. It was as though she was right at home among the chaos. Her parents had walked her through all of the booths where people were set up selling stuffed animals and snacks of all kind. Bo and Annie had already bought her a big ice drink, a large stuffed lion, and a light up stick that had top hats swirling around it. When they all got to their seats, it didn't take Jenny too long to realize that she had a few rows of people in front of her that were blocking her from being able to see certain sections of the tent.

Jenny finally blew her top, "I want to see! There's too many big tall people in front of me and it's making me so mad!" she shouted.

"Why don't you come over here and sit on my lap or I can even hold you on my shoulders," offered Bo.

"I don't want to sit there! That's not my seat! I want my own seat!" People began looking as Jenny set her attention on a little girl in the front row of seats. "I want the seat that little girl has."

"Jenny, calm down. Please. We'll have to leave."

"I don't want to leave, I want to see!" Jenny got so outraged that she slung her ice drink out towards where the girl was sitting. Fortunately for the other little girl, Jenny didn't have too good of a depth of perception when she was five. However, this would too prove unfortunate for the gray haired woman in front of her.

The family was forced to leave the circus and the gray haired woman filed a law suit against the family. She tried to say that she was being harassed, but since it was such a young child, the lawsuit was thrown out the window before anyone even stepped foot in a lawyers office. This was the needle in the haystack that many people were hoping that the two parents would find. Could it really be possible that their little angel, wasn't so much of an angel after all? Could it really be possible that maybe their strategy on giving a kid all of their hearts desires would wind up being just as bad as having not given their daughter anything at all?

Jenny grew older, but her same 'only child' mentality remained. What her parents had engrained in her for the first five years of her life, skewed her perception of the world and what the world should have to offer up to her. She always kept a good relationship with her parents, though. It would be someone insane not to keep a good relationship with your parents when they spend countless dollars on you.

She made the honor roll all throughout high school. This wasn't because she was a fantastic student, by any means. What it did mean, is she knew what certain teachers wanted, and knew how to wrap herself around their fingers. With the men, that usually mean spending some time after school to gain 'extra credit'. She even had really good relationships with her female teachers, not because she would let a little skin show, but because she would always get a little brown on her nose. She knew how to flatter. Regardless of gender, she could always make someone reach out and give her a hand. Even if it mean shed use it just to step on them in the future.

When she went to college she decided that studying was not her calling. She was supposed to be a star. Sadly, in order to get to stardom, one must possess some sort of talent to make people around them interested. Jenny wasn't a multi talented girl, she wasn't even a talented girl to say the least. She decided that she would take an initiative to enter the modeling world. Even though she was a beautiful girl, her voluptuousness would hold her back from ever truly making a mark on an industry that thrives off of girls who are as tall as skyscrapers, but as thin as a pencil.

The only kind of modeling work that Jenny could get was glamor work. Often she would only be paid with photos, but on some occasion when she'd show a little more skin, she'd be paid with Benjamin's. It was almost an epiphany the first time that she was given money for letting a photographer see her birthday suit. It was then that she realized that she had a little more to offer the world than she thought. She enjoyed men, but most of all she enjoyed spending their money.

Jenny found herself a job working nights at a local strip club. The men loved her, simply because of her realness. She wasn't a size zero, and her boobs were real bouncy jugs, not rocks that had been established long after puberty. One day a man in his fifties found himself more than interested in the girl. He knew that she was worth more than the being the stripper at some scummy club. Being a wealthy man, he was able to have Jenny wrap herself around his little finger.

They got married within the first few months of meeting each other. Even though he knew that she was solely attached to him for his money, he knew that she would be around. As long as the money would flow, so would her interest in him. He would take Jenny everywhere that her heart desired. Europe was one of their favorite destination spots, Milan in particular. When you're married to a girl like Jenny, shoes aren't an uncommon item to need countless supplies of.

A few years passed by and Jenny began to bore of her husband. Her husband was aging and he had lost a good bit of muscle mass within the three previous year and in place had stacked a spare tire. Jenny stayed with him of course, she had no money to her own name and had to survive somehow. She still would force herself to enjoy his company, simply because she knew how much she enjoyed the company of his money.

One day when Jenny was at a local designer shoe store she came across a good looking man in his late twenties, not too much older than Jenny. While she was standing by some shoes on the wall he glanced up from where he was eying a pair of shoes, and caught her eye, "Well, hello."

Jenny, caught off guard by his good looks said, "Hello handsome."

They both blushed as he walked over to her, "I'm Phillip."

"I'm sorry, I'm Jenny."

"No need to be sorry, Jenny. I like that you think I'm handsome."

"I'm not sure if this is appropriate."

"What? I'm in a shoe store, you're in a shoe store."

"I'm married, sorry."

"I didn't ask if you were or not."

Jenny stared at the mysterious man for a solid minute before realizing that she may have just found someone who could size her up. "Alright then Phillip. You enjoy buying stilettos often?"

"They're not for me," he said.

"I assumed. That wasn't what I was getting at."

"Of course not, but I would love to buy the pair you've been eyeballing for the past fifteen minutes."

"You do, do you?" she looked Phillip up and down and answered her own question, "So you do. I'm thirsty. How about you buy me a drink as well?"

"I'd love that."

Jenny, married, allowed Phillip, also married, to buy her a nice pair of designer shoes that would tip the bank at two thousand dollars. Men with standards usually come with women with standards that don't remain physical, but monetary. They went to a nearby restaurant to have drinks.

"So," asked Phillip, "What does your husband do?"

"He is a CEO of a highly ranked phone service company. How about your wife?" she asked as she took a long sip of her martini.

"Stay at home mom."

"Ah, you have kids then," she said downing her drink. "I could possibly rattle a house, but I don't think I could wreck a home. I appreciate the drink, but I have to leave," she said as she shifted in her bar stool to reach the purse on the hook under the bar.

"I never said I wanted you to wreck my home. I would never want you anywhere near my home. All I was hoping for, was a little fun. Just you and me. No one would ever know," he said as he reached for her hand to sit back down.

She placed her hand in his and sat back down, "You have me interested."

"It wouldn't be a permanent thing of course. I have my own life, and you have yours, I'm sure." She nodded and he continued, "I'd like to spend money on you. Treat you like a woman like you deserves to be treated. I have a wife at home, whom I love dearly, but occasionally it's nice to feed a neighboring pet before sending it on it's way home."

"What are you suggesting?"

"I own a cabin in Aspen. Not so much a cabin, as it is a four thousand square foot chalet over looking the valleys and good shopping centers below." He stared at her and when he could tell she was waiting for him to continue, he did, "I would like for you to fly out with me to my cabin. I assume you don't have any children, so there would be no need for a babysitter. I would cover the cost of your ticket so there would be no worries there."

"I have my own money Phillip."

"Yes, but like I said, I like to feed my neighbors pets occasionally. I'll take care of anything needed money wise for this trip."

"What would I tell my husband?"

"He's away quite often for business isn't he?" Jenny nodded and he continued giving options, "Well, if he does happen to have plans to stay home this weekend, tell him that you're flying off to Aspen to visit a friend of yours who you haven't seen in ages. Technically it wouldn't be lying. He would know exactly where you were going, and know that you were going to meet up with someone. You wouldn't have even told him that it was a girl you were meeting up with. Simply an 'old friend'. If you're the kind to worry about your conscious, which I assume you're not, you wouldn't have lied to your husband about anything, really."

"This all sounds very tempting, but what about your wife and kids?" She rested her head in her hand and continued, "Don't you think your wife probably suspects something goes on when you take weekend trips to Aspen?"

"No, not really. She tends to the children, but she has full reliability in me. I pay for everything she could ever need. My company is primarily here, however we also have a branch out in Aspen. Work is there. Whether she actually believes that I go there occasionally for the weekend on business is another story. I think she probably has the idea that something goes on when I'm out there, but she's fully satisfied with everything at home, and I give her everything her heart could desire, so I'm not quite sure that she would really find offense to it."

"I've never done anything like this before. You shouldn't assume that I'm a whore if I take you up on the offer."

"Never said you were a whore. I would put you more in the category of digging for gold, but definitely not a whore."

"Excuse me?" she said, bruised.

"I didn't mean it in a bad way, I like that in a woman. Some women have no clue what they want out of life, I can respect a lady having her eye set on something and going after what she wants."

"You may not be the most charming man I've ever laid interest in, but you are a fairly smart one."

"Good then," he said as he pulled a business card from his wallet, "This is my work email address. No one can get into the account but me. Email me when you get the chance. I'll arrange your plane flight for you and email you the confirmation for it."

"Thank you," she said as she pocketed the business card."

"Here's something you can expect over the weekend," and he leaned in to kiss her.

That evening her husband walked in the front door as she was sending an email to Phillip, "Where are you Jenny?"

"Shit," she mumbled to herself. "I'm up here," she said as she exited her email account."

He walked up the stairs and made his way to her study, which was basically her bedroom. Occasionally they would sleep in the same bed, but many nights she would fall asleep watching TV on the day bed in the room. If she ever woke up in the middle of the night she would just lay there, rather than going and crawling in her marital bed. There was nothing there of interest to her anyway.

"I have a grand idea dear," he said as he pulled up a chair next to her, "I have to go to New York for a meeting this weekend, and I was thinking that I'd take you with me."

"Oh," she said disappointed, "This weekend?"

"Yes," he said confused, "I thought I could take you with me and we could spend the weekend shopping, maybe see a little Broadway."

"That sounds like it would be amazing, but I sort of made plans for myself for the weekend already."

"Doing what?"

"Well, an old friend of mine," she searched through her mind for the right words, "one I practically haven't seen in forever, invited me to Aspen."

"Oh, Aspen. My that sounds nice. Maybe I could just reschedule my appointment this weekend in New York and I could go with you. Then we could have two weekends to spend time together and reconnect."

She patted his check with her right hand and said, "That sounds like it would be wonderful, but she just recently got divorced. I think it would be rude to take my fabulous husband with me. Somewhat rubbing it in her face."

"I see, I wouldn't want to be a spare wheel anyways. I'll go to my meeting in New York then. You have fun in Aspen." He stared at her and pulled away from her arm on his shoulder. "You finish doing whatever you're up to. I'll be downstairs having a drink."

"I'll be down there shortly to join you," she said with a smirk as he left the room.

Jenny reopened her email to Phillip. She quickly typed out all of the information that he would need to buy her ticket. The week leading up to her flight she had feelings of guilt. Although she'd often thought of what it would be like to be with someone other than her husband, she could never allow herself to think out the process of what would ensue. She only had thought about how nice it might be to someday be able to have someone decent looking around to spend time with. When she would catch herself daydreaming of things like this, she would try her damnedest to reroute her train of thought. She knew that anyone her age would most likely still be climbing the ladder of employment. They wouldn't be fully stable until they were the age that her husband was.

She told herself that this wouldn't be a long term commitment. She and Phillip had an arrangement. He would spend money lavishly on her, as long as she flew out to spend time with him. To many this situation would seem odd. However, to those with money, not so much. In her community she never had too many friends. She had them growing up, but as she grew older she found it more and more difficult to retain them. She didn't need someone to sit around and talk with. The ones she talked with often were put off by her selfish nature, and eventually would disappear from Jenny's life. Once she got married, many people had distaste for the age gap between her husband and her. Jenny wasn't too worried by this, she only wanted two things out of life: to live happy and have money. As far as she was concerned those were interchangeable. She couldn't have happiness without money, and she couldn't have money without having some form of happiness. She assumed that she would find, at least for a small period of time, a friend. The relationship wouldn't last longer than a weekend, but it would bring her happiness, and in turn money.

It was the day of her flight out to meet Phillip. Jenny packed two large suitcases for an eventful sum of two days. She wasn't sure what her lover would have up his sleeve, so she brought along a few things just in case. One suitcase contained nothing but makeup and hair supplies. The other was bag was filled half way with clothes and shoes. She made sure to save room in her luggage so that she would have somewhere to put the gifts that Phillip would buy her. He had insisted that she would be pampered, so she wanted to ensure that she would be prepared.

Jenny and her husband's flights were departing only an hour apart, so he insisted that she ride with him to the airport. When he went to lift her suitcases into the trunk of the town car he noticed how light they felt in comparison to any luggage she would pack when they went on vacation.

"Jenny, these bags are pretty light. What, did you only pack your makeup this time?" asked her husband.

"No, I just wanted to save some room for things I'm going to buy while I'm in Aspen."

"Ah, I see. Well get whatever your heart desires."

She intended on doing just that. Once they were both at the airport, her husband kissed her goodbye and went to go hop on his plane. Jenny watched her husband walk away, and was overwhelmed with the happiness and excitement for the weekend ahead of her. No longer would she have to put up with the spare tire and bad breath of her husband.

At the check in line, Jenny was welcomed by a young girl with her hair back in a ponytail, "I'm sorry ma'am," she said as she tried to pull up Jenny's information. "It looks as though your plane has been canceled."

"Excuse me?" Jenny asked the girl.

"Aspen has been experiencing many plane cancellations due to blizzards. The planes simply can't get out."

"Is there any way you could re-route me?"

"Well, we do have a plane coming down from Connecticut that will layover here and then depart for Aspen, but it takes off about two hours after your plane would've departed."

"That's fine," said Jenny.

The attendant at the check in counter gave her all of the information she would need to get on the plane. Jenny went to the gate and as she sat there she became uneasy within herself. She had thoughts of regret and guilt racing through her mind. Would her husband find out that she wasn't really meeting an old friend, but instead was going to meet up with some man who was practically a stranger? What if this man was a lunatic? He seemed fairly normal, but who can really tell what normal is from abnormal. Especially after only two drinks and email encounters.

Her worries subsided as the flight attendants called out that boarding would begin soon. The young mothers and elderly went first. Then there were a few other sections to board before she would be allowed to board on the plane. Finally when she got in line to board the plane she stood behind a couple holding hands with their wedding bands on. She couldn't help but wonder whether they were actually married to one another or not. It's a mis-assumption that everyone who holds hands and wears wedding bands are married. What about two people who are cheating on their spouses? They would likely still have their wedding bands on. It would be an easy way to not attract attention. Many take their wedding bands off, but to simply leave them on takes full judgment away from onlookers with judgmental beliefs.

She finally made her way onto the plane and stowed her carry-on above her head. Though she wasn't going to be gone too long, she wanted to make sure she brought some makeup on the plane with her for touch-ups. She also made sure that she brought her laptop along in case Phillip ended up being one of those men who enjoys his alone time. Just because he was flying her out to spend time and money on, didn't mean that he wasn't going to want his space. Some men are just strange that way.

The flight attendants came on the overhead stereo system. The plane began to taxi the runway, and the flight attendants told the passengers that they would be taking off shortly. She gave everyone the rundown of what each passenger would need to do in the event that anything unexpected happened. Jenny always thought that these talks were unnecessary. She'd flown many times without there being anything more than turbulence. Sometimes the turbulence would worry her, but she had never needed to use the oxygen masks. By the time anything unexpected would begin to happen, did people really even have the capacity to remain calm enough to take the right precautions?

The plane had taken off and had been flying for about an hour when the pilot came across the plane overhead system, "Passengers, please buckle up. We're in for a bumpy ride. We have been told by the Air Traffic Control tower near the Aspen airport that there has been horrible icing due to the blizzard on the tarmac. On top of that there is an unusual air gust that we will be flying through."

The pilot turned off the overhead radio system and the passengers all buckled up. The turbulence began not even a minute after the pilot had gotten off the radio. At first the bumps seemed like the usual turbulence that Jenny had remembered. Five minutes later they were still dealing with turbulence, but it was getting worse. They hit a large air gust that sent the plane leaning heavy to the left. The pilot tried to compensate by pulling strongly to the right, but when he did it was too hard of a pull. The plane began to spin until it was upside down. Oxygen masks were falling out of their compartments. Once again the pilot tried his damnedest to get the plane back on it's stomach, but the plane began descending at a sharp decline. Passengers, Jenny included, began passing out from the shock to the body that the descend was causing. Despite the efforts of the pilot and co-pilot, the plane was never able to regain stability. It took four minutes for the plane to crash in a valley nearby the Aspen airport.

Five

It was nine thirty on a Tuesday night. Laura Bates had been working a double shift since eight o'clock that morning. She was not only a workaholic, but a perfectionist student at the local university. This year she had finally determined that she was meant to be a lawyer. It took her three years of shifting through different majors for her to finally land on her ultimate decision. Originally when she went to school she was determined that biology was the field for her. Anything to do with animals or the study of them peaked her interest. Though, when it came down to the dissection of animals, Laura was unable to cut open the aborted baby pig. Due to the many dissections that she would have to do to gain her degree, she determined that this might not be the right route for her. Her second year of college she thought she might want to go to veterinary school. For reasons unknown, she didn't piece together the fact that at some point she would have to, once again, do dissections in order to learn the anatomy of animals. When a cat that had died of diabetes was placed on the counter in front of her to dissect, she vomited in the nearest trash receptacle and took off to the counselors office, to once again get her major changed.

At first they switched her major to a simple general studies degree. That was until the next summer when she finally had hit the degree jackpot. She knew that her life was meant to be built around the lives of animals. They were her utmost interest, and she was a long time vegan. Laura knew that she would never be able to be a vet because it would mean that she would have to deal with the occasional euthanasia. She also knew that she would never be able to major in biology because she couldn't stomach dissections. There was one career she could do that would, at some point or another: aid animals. Being an animal rights lawyer, she would be able to help the lives of many abused animals, without having to cut open any animals during her college career. In fact, it was likely that she would be able to more greatly impact the lives of more animals than her previous two majors.

Because of the fact that she was going for a law degree, she would have to make sure that her grades were at the top of not only her class, but at the top of the grades and scores of everyone else studying law. She wanted to be taken seriously. All of her life was built around being taken seriously. Being gorgeous made it even more difficult for people to see the brains beneath her beautiful scalp. Often times people would remark, 'Oh you have looks that you'll always be able to fall back on, lucky you'. She was always trying her best to prove that she was much more than beauty. Though she and the ones closest to her knew that she was a double threat, having a law degree would prove it to those who were at a distance.

Working at a restaurant was the easiest way to have a flexible work schedule that would still allow her to make a little side money. She had classes Monday, Wednesday, and Friday. Her classes were all morning classes, which she would be done with by two each afternoon. Many students in college wont take classes early in the morning because they want to be able to stay up late partying. Occasionally she would do a little partying herself, but she would always make sure that she wouldn't get so trashed that she wouldn't be able to wake up the next morning for her seven o'clock class. She went to college to actually go to college. She would work Friday and Saturday nights at the restaurant she worked at, and occasionally on the weekdays she didn't have classes she would pull doubles. It was killing time to her. She would study her ass off on the other days, and working gave her something to do. The group of friends she circled in were all study-holics, so her lifestyle meshed perfectly with theirs.

Spring break was coming up quickly and Laura and her friends wanted to escape from college and their studies for a week, in celebration of all their hard work. Midterms had just passed and they had all aced their examinations. None of them had enjoyed a study free day since Christmas. It was time for them to let loose and let their hair down. The Friday before spring break the four friends got together in one of their dorms for a girls night.

In the midst of painting nails, Laura spoke up, "You know what we need?"

"What's that?" asked Becky.

"We need," Laura started as she sat up on the bed, "to get away. Somewhere close, but far enough away so that we can forget about this place for a while."

"Like where?" asked Julie, "I mean, spring break is a week long, but I personally can't afford a plane ticket anywhere."

"And after that plane just crashed in Aspen, I'm in no hurry whatsoever to fly anywhere," said Anna.

"Oh please, it's one plane," Laura said

"Yeah but they can't figure out anything that went wrong. Totally shady," rebuttalled Anna.

"So we road trip it. I mean think about it guys, we live in Tennessee. We're only a day's drive away from Panama City."

"I guess that could be fun," Anna said as the other two girls nodded in agreement.

"Alright, I'll look out online to see if there are any hotel deals for the week." Laura got on her laptop and started searching, almost instantly she found a deal that would work perfectly for the four girls. "Aha! I found it. Get this girls," she gestured for them to listen up, "One hotel room with two full size beds, right on the beach, only 60 bucks a night. Not even in a shady part of Panama City Beach."

"Uhm," thought Julia, "Isn't all of Panama City a little shady?"

"Yes! Not the point though, the point is," continued Laura, "that we're going to the beach, and by the time we split the hotel room, it'll only cost us fifteen dollars a night. We split the gas cost and drive down tomorrow and drive back next Saturday."

"Sounds good to me," said Becky.

"Alrighty, then. I say we all pack some stuff and meet back here. Then we can all get up in the morning and drive out," Laura insisted.

All of the girls went to their separate dorms to quickly pack some belongings. After busting her ass at work, Laura was able to go on a vacation with her girlfriends without even having to break the bank. Being the workaholic that she is, she realized that the trip would really only cost each of them a few hundred dollars, including food and beer. She would even have a good bit of her cash stashed away for when she got back, even if she did for some reason splurge a little.

Once the girls got back to the room they all shared a bottle of wine and easily drifted off to sleep. The girls woke up and got their things in the car and headed off to the beach. On the way down there they switched off so that no one girl would be stuck doing all of the driving. They only had about a ten hour drive, but they still wanted to be sure that they were fully energized for a week of fun at the beach.

As Julia started driving, Becky and Anna dozed off in the back seat. Laura and Julia, got to talking about boys in their lives and relationship situations they were in. Julia asked Laura about her relationship status with her long time boyfriend, "So, are you two still, you know?"

"I guess," she thought for a second, "I mean I'm not sure really."

"How are you not sure? Usually if you're in a relationship with someone you'd know."

"Well, we dated for years. Even in high school, you know?" Julia nodded and Laura continued, "It just seems like we're growing more apart than we are together."

"You're young, you know? You have a lifetime ahead of you."

"I get that. I think it's more that the strings from our past are holding us together than anything we've got going on now."

"I totally get where you're coming from. Me and my ex finally had to break things off this past Thanksgiving. He was going to be going home from college to visit family, and I didn't want to because it was only a two day break for us, and even though that would had given me two more days with the weekend, I just didn't want to drive home for that short of time."

"He must taken that pretty hard."

"Yeah, but honestly it made me realize that I wasn't that interested in our relationship anymore. Like, if I really had been as into it as I was when we were younger, there would've been nothing stopping me from going to see him. It just hit me that I wasn't really all that into him anymore." Julia took her eye off the road a quick minute to analyze her friend in the passenger seat next to her, "Want to know something between you and me?" She put her eyes back on the road and waited for her friend to respond.

"What's that?"

"I don't think you would've even thought about wanting to get away from campus if you were really that interested in him. I mean, yeah you guys have been together four years now and somehow managed to make it into the same college as each other, but if you really were up for being with him, why would you have decided to jet off on the only time you would have been willing to take a break from studying?"

"Not too sure, girl. I mean," Laura lifted her seat back up from a laying position and fixed her seat belt before continuing, "we care about each other, but we know we have our own things going on. We're just drifting apart I think."

"Well, let me ask you something," said Julia, "do you even know what he's doing for spring break? Or even bother to tell him what you're doing?"

"No," she let it marinate for a minute before letting out a huge chuckle, "holy crap. I don't think he and I are dating anymore. The last time we talked to each other was last week and it was just to check in."

"Haha, wow, OK. yeah. So how's about we get our asses to the beach for some total girl time fun," said Julia as they crossed the Georgia and Florida state border.

The four girls finally made their way to the hotel they were staying at. After they parked their car, they grabbed their belongings and made their way towards the lobby of the hotel. They realized that even for a group of college girls, this place wasn't too shabby. It smelled like cocoa butter and coconuts, just as the beach should smell. Everything looked pristine as though it had been cleaned just before they walked inside. The hotel had enclosed hallways, so it wasn't like they were staying at some shady motel.

Since Laura was the one who booked the room, she went to check in.

"Name, please?" asked the clerk behind the counter.

"Laura Bates."

The clerk pulled up her information, "Aaalright, Ms. Bates. Room 205 will be the room you and your friends will be staying in. It is on the beach side of the hotel, and has a balcony."

"That sounds wonderful."

"We do have a policy here," the clerk said as she stared between the girls. "Quiet hours begin at ten in the evening and let up at six in the morning. No drugs or paraphernalia, of course, and no rowdiness as we are a family hotel."

Laura felt as though she was being judged by the older woman. Rather than being a complete smart ass, she simply brushed off anything the clerk was implying off of her shoulders, "No problem," she said with a huge smile.

"Goodness," said the woman, "you surely are gorgeous. Aren't you lucky."

That stung, always being told she was beautiful, and never being fully looked at for her brains. She always wanted her brains to be apart of the package. Even though they naturally were, it usually wasn't seen by the outside world, only those close to her.

"Thank you, ma'am," Laura said as she and her friends got ready to head up to their room.

They rounded the hallways and made their way up the elevator. When they finally got to their room they went inside. It was much nicer than any of them had assumed they would've been able to get for sixty bucks. Then again, this was a party town and they had found a deal at the fast handed searching skills of Laura.

"So," said Laura, "I'm famished."

"Ugh, me too," said Becky as she threw herself on the bed. "A little tired too."

"Tired," exclaimed Julia, "You slept nearly the whole drive down, how could you be tired?"

"I say we spruce up a little and head out for some drinks and grub," offered Laura.

The girls all agreed that, that sounded like an amazing plan. Each of them took turns in the shower, and reapplied their makeup. They got dressed to the nines, at least for beach wear, and got ready for their first night out on the town. It was the first time for them to get away from campus. Getting away from campus meant leaving behind the worries of grades or boys. At least the boys that they were used to seeing around the town they went to college in.

Each of them had made a pact on the way down to Panama City Beach. They had decided that no matter how gorgeous the guy, none of them would have a hook up. None whatsoever. This was a trip to get away from their worries, and oddly enough, men just complicated life and created drama; at least for college aged girls. This was a trip for rejuvenation. Where they could let loose for once and have no worries in the world. Not even a care to what some good looking hunk may think of what they're doing. The trip was intended to get back to their true selves, the ones they may have drifted away from while they were studying their asses off, or the one they lost trying to impress some boy.

Being out in a party town proved difficult for any of them to be invisible to the opposite sex. Nearly everywhere they went there were groups of guys offering to buy them shots or little cute drinks with umbrellas in them. They would take the drinks of course, they weren't so stupid as to waste a good free drink, however they would just share a nod and a wink with the person who bought them the drink. Nothing more.

After having a few drinks and wandering up and down the beach together, it had grown dark outside. The girls decided it was a good time as any to go ahead and turn in. They'd driven all day and were beat from not only the drive, but the late nights studying the previous week. Throughout the next few days they spent their time meandering the beach and soaking up rays. Occasionally one of them would wake up from sun bathing and start talking to their friends.

"You guys, I'm feeling roasted," said Laura.

"That's because you are roasted," said Anna.

Julia and Becky looked up from the towels they were sun bathing on. The look on their faces was somewhat reminiscent of a mixture between being horrified and in pain.

"Holy crap, maybe we should go inside for a little while," said Laura.

"You know there's this cool oddities museum along the main strip." Becky said, "I've wanted to go there, but never have had the chance when I've stayed here. It's all indoors and Laura the Lobster would be able to have some time out of the sun."

"Before we go rub some of this aloe on, the sooner you use it, the better." Julia tossed Laura the tube of aloe vera from her bag.

The girls grabbed their belongings and threw their coverups over their swimsuits. They waited as Laura rubbed the lotion on her skin. Then she put her clothes on again. As they walked up the beach they couldn't help but realize how many good looking guys there were. A lot of them were with good looking girls of course, but there were just as many good looking ones without girlfriends hanging off of their arms.

When the girls reached the oddity museum they were ready for some cool air. The line was wrapped around the building as other people waited to go into the tourist trap. Once inside they realized this tourist attraction wasn't one of the cheapest ones in town. It was something to do though, and allowed them to get a little outside of their box.

"Hey guys," whispered Julia. "I grabbed these from the room's minibar this morning. Figured they'd come in handy. Looks like they will."

"There's twelve of those," said Laura.

"You, my dear should have been a math major," Julia retorted.

"I don't think that was her point, those things are like six dollars a shot," said Anna.

"So we split the cost, like we have been doing the whole trip," offered Julia.

The girls took the shots quickly, before anyone could assume anything and kept walking through the museum. There were little artifacts in glass boxes with captions beside them claiming strange things such as, 'hair from the first bearded woman' and rooms of mirrors where people could easily get vertigo from the lack of direction.

When they were in the middle of one of the mirrored rooms Laura thought she saw someone she recognized, "Guys, is that Josh?"

"What? Where?" asked Julia as the girls looked around.

"He was just there," Laura hesitated and realized the shots mixed with the sunburn she had acquired this morning may have made her hallucinate her 'somewhat boyfriend' a quick second. "Never mind, must've just been someone who looked like him."

"Alright," said Anna, "today is the last day we are boy free. Tonight when some cutie buys us a drink, we're going to dance with them. Some male interaction. We're obviously deprived."

That night the girls had a blast dancing the night away. They all had good looking dance partners, as they were all great looking girls. When the night was finally over and they had enough of the make out sessions with strangers, the girls all headed back to the hotel room. Once they were back there, they all sat out on the balcony letting their damp hair dry after washing away the musk of the day.

"This has really been the best vacation I've ever had," said Laura.

"I would hope so," said Julia, "it was your idea in the first place."

"Honestly, I wasn't so sure it would've been so much fun, I just wanted to get away from all the studying and madness of college."

They all did. Whether or not in that moment on the balcony they would admit it, they were all ready to be done with college and it's madness. The constant want of partying, the constant worrying of grades, the constant struggle of studying. It was only one more full year before they would be out in the real world. One more year of college and they would be on with their lives. College for them, as it is for most, is very similar to high school. The only difference is that the grades you make in college can really impact how your career takes off. The other aspects are identical. There's the initial worry over the newness, being the newness. There's the constant wanting to 'fit in', even though in the end you'll just end up working on opposite ends of the country from your friends and hardly get the chance to catch up on the happenings in their life.

The next morning was their last full day in Panama City Beach. The trip had been symbolic of a lot that the girls had gone through in their college careers. Simply put, they had chose to take the more wise path in college. Instead of being sorority sisters and partying every night, they chose to study their asses off so that they could actually be able to pave a path for their life. Through studying hard, they had earned one of the best weeks of their lives, and really were able to appreciate it. They all got to the beach and laid out their towels. When they were putting sunscreen on, Julia looked up from beneath her sunglasses, "Oh shit."

The other girls looked in the direction she was looking and noticed what was leaving her speechless. All in all, Laura wasn't hallucinating her ex the day before. Apparently he had managed to be on the same beach and stumbling across the same footsteps that Laura was. Only, Josh wasn't down here for a week with his buddies. He was down for a week with a tan, bleached blonde barbie.

"Hey Asshole!" Julia shouted.

Josh turned around, "Fuck," he mumbled to himself. He tried to keep walking, but his new play toy stopped him.

"What's going on?" the girl asked him.

"My ex's psycho friends."

Laura walked up to him, "Would've been nice to have known we were officially ex's."

"So what, am I, like, the whore now?" asked the blonde bimbo.

"No," said Laura, "technically not. We weren't really even dating the last few weeks. I guess I loved the shadow of Josh for a few years, but that was before he turned into a loser who cared about nothing more than drinking and drugging." Laura noticed him staring at his new girlfriend's chest. "Too bad he didn't have the same passion for school as he does your silicone."

Laura took Julia by the arm, and lead her back to her friends who were sitting on their beach towels. As they sat down they realized Josh and his new girlfriend were going into the water in front of them. Once they had gotten a few yards out the girl took her bikini top off and looked back in the direction of the group of girls. She then took his face in her hands and began kissing him.

"What a hoe," said Julia.

"I hope she gives him an STD," Laura said, as she started busting out laughing. The girls all lifted their beers up to one another and took a swig. "Here's to our loser ex's. May they all find someone as dimwitted and trashy as that girl."

Just then they heard a blood curling shriek. They looked to where the scream came from and it was the trashy blonde who had released it.

"What the hell," said Julia.

"HELP!" The girl shouted, "It's a shark!"

Josh and the girl swam furiously to the shore, the girl having to help with his weight as he'd been the one the shark went after. Laura ran over to the water's edge to help the girl. When she'd gotten ankle deep she saw why he was leaning so heavily on the girl. The shark had ripped off his left leg, all the way up to the point where the hamstring meets the pelvis. Laura and the girl laid him down on the sand. People were rushing up, encircling Josh. Whether they were going to try to help, or were simply trying to see what was causing a commotion was questionable.

Finally a few lifeguards had came down by the water to help. By the time they'd reached them it was too late. It took five minutes from the second the shark ripped his leg off for him to bleed out.

Six

Tony Dinito grew up in a wealthy Italian-American family. His dad made good enough money that his mother wouldn't have to work a day in her life. The family was set. Not only did little Tony's family make a decent amount of money, but so did the extended members of his family. The Original Dinito's sailed over from Sicily back in 1890. Mrs. Dinito was pregnant with two little twin boys as they made their way across the Atlantic. Those boy's would grow up to raise their own children and grandchildren. One of the great-grandchildren of the immigrants was little Tony. Although his ancestors were long gone before he made an arrival, Tony still grew up with the gratitude of the Italian heritage, as well as an open heart and warm embrace of the American lifestyle. Tony's parents were able to give him the American dream that their grandparents had traveled so far for them to be able to obtain.

Occasionally the Dinito's would find it hard to make ends meet. That wouldn't stop them from living life as dreamers. One day when Tony's dad was down on his luck, his uncle offered him some help.

"You know," said his uncle, "there is a way to get out of all this shit your in."

"Like what?" his dad asked him, already knowing what his offer would be. Tony's uncle had always struggled with substance abuse addiction, and although the family usually looked the other way, they all knew he had a problem.

"I know this guy who needs some things moved. You move them, and I'm sure you'd be set for a while."

Tony's dad did the job, and even though he would've been set for life off of that one job, he got money hungry. Eventually Tony's dad and uncle 'offed someone who was moving a lot of the cocaine in the state, and they began distributing it in his place. The Dinito's always had a pact that the industry would end with their generation. They would never want their sons or daughters having to work the way they had to. Pushing drugs was dangerous business, and even though they were already putting their sons in danger, they didn't want them to have to follow in their footsteps.

The children in the family went to good schools. Each of them went to private schools in state and their grades were kept up with regularly. It was rare for any of them to make less than an 'A'. On occasion little Tony would feel the pressure of having good grades eat away at him. It wasn't that he wasn't capable of maintaining a certain grade point average, because he was wise beyond means. He knew what his grades meant to his parents. It was everything to them, even though he just assumed it was because it would make them look good. Little did he know that his family strived for the children to do well in school so that they wouldn't have to fall into the same line of work that the parents did.

Trafficking drugs is something that would be difficult to hide from growing children. Tony's dad and uncle would dress up in suits and fly out for 'business trips'. He never quite knew what they did for a living, as every time he would ask them, they'd say something like, 'Oh we work in funds'. His dad was never gone too long, so he never really questioned what he did for a living. Who really ever questions what their parents do for a living?

A few weeks after starting college, Tony came home to visit his parents for the weekend. When he opened the door he found blood spatters across the walls. Horrified, he stood there for a good five minutes before entering his childhood home. Finally he pushed himself through the entrance way and around to the living room where they had movie night when he was a boy. There he found his mom laying on the ground, face to the floor. He ran over to his mom and kneeled down at her side. Laying there he felt a breeze coming through the sliding patio door. Tony stood up after giving his mom a kiss on the head and ran out the back door. His dad was in the pool, where his blood spilled, mixing in with the chlorine water. He didn't know what to do when he heard a voice coming from behind him.

"I think I should explain a few things to you," said his Uncle Denny.

"Call the cops! You can explain whatever it is later," Tony said.

"We can't call the cops."

"Why the hell can't we?"

"There's something you didn't know about the lifestyle your family had," said his uncle as he gestured towards the patio chairs. When they had both sat down, he continued, "There was a point in time when your dad and I were struggling financially. I had a battle with substance abuse and knew some guys who needed hands with some," he hesitated, "shares. It was good money, and we could've been set on that alone, but instead, we kept our hands in the pot of money."

"You're the reason why my parent's are dead."

"I can't deny that. But I can say that there were definitely dangers, which your dad was well aware of."

"I'm going to call the cops. I really don't give a damn if they come get you, Denny."

"It's not me you have to worry about them getting, it's the people who are going to come get you, if they find out you were the one who called."

"Then they wont find out I called, now will they?" He stood up and went to go grab the house phone.

"I wouldn't do that if I were you. They're going to know it was their son. Who else would come out here and call the cops? It sure as hell wouldn't have been me."

"What the hell do we do then?" asked Tony, confused shitless.

"We clean shit up."

Tony stood there speechless. He debated whether or not to give his uncle the middle finger and race toward the phone, or help him clean up his parent's blood bath. It only took three minutes for him to realize that he'd rather be in trouble with the cops, than in trouble with the assholes who did this to his parents. "Fuck. Fine, whatever," Tony told his uncle as they headed into the kitchen for cleaning supplies.

They cleaned up for the next few hours. It was obvious to Tony that this wasn't his uncle's first time having to deal with the clean up of a dead body. He handled everything in a way that only a professional could. When they were done Tony began to realize that something would have to be done with the bodies of his parents. Certainly, his uncle couldn't be so heartless as to just dump them off somewhere. Of course, Tony didn't really know his uncle as well as he thought he did.

The two of them bagged up his parents' bodies and drove out to an old rock quarry. There hadn't been any rock mining done there in a good decade or two, so they wouldn't have to worry about any unexpected visitors. In fact, Tony's uncle made sure to let him know that this wasn't the first time he's been here, so there shouldn't be anything to worry about. As far as modern day technology, this place was off of the map.

On their drive back home, Uncle Denny struck up a conversation with Tony. "You do realize that with your parents gone, there are some shoes to fill."

"I know," said Tony. "I was the oldest out of my brothers and sisters."

"That's not what I meant," said Uncle Denny, as he leaned in towards the stereo to turn the volume down.

Catching his drift, Tony got pissed, "You're out of your damn mind. First you get my dad into all of this mess, then he gets killed. The day he dies and we clean up the whole mess you really expect me to jump on the whole drug boat?"

"I'm not saying that you have to stay on the boat forever, but what I do know is that your dad had one last job to do. He was going to do this job with me and we were going to be done with the crap."

"What was the job?" asked Tony as he looked down at the floorboard. He wasn't sure if it was because he'd just dealt with the most bizarre day of his life, or if it was the fact that he wanted to finish what is dad started, but he was somewhat interested in what the job was.

"One last run. If not for the money, then for your dad's sake. A finishing off, of sorts."

"Where to?"

"Vegas."

"Sounds a bit cliche to me."

"What?"

"A drug run to Vegas."

"Look," Uncle Denny said, getting pissed and then controlling his anger, "I know you're dealing with a lot of crap right now. But look, we do the job and it's done. Everything. Your mom and pops didn't die in vain. Finish the job, and you could retire in Panama City, having a wild party for the rest of your life."

"I've never been much of a party boy, plus isn't that where the kid I went to school with just got his leg ripped off?"

"Not my fault you decided to go down south for schooling. Not my fault you knew the guy. That's all besides the point. Are you in, or not?"

Tony considered his options. He didn't want to be apart of anything his newly shady uncle had up his sleeve. Then again, he didn't want to send himself down a path of uncertain death by some drug overlord. "I'm in," he told his uncle.

"Damn straight. I knew you wouldn't leave me on a hook."

"Under one condition." He waited for his uncle to nod, and when he did, Tony continued, "No one ever finds out about dad's real job. My parents are considered missing, no one even finds out we found them. Most important, I'm not stuck in the damn lifestyle you and dad chose for yourselves."

"Fine by me. We leave in the morning."

The next morning the pair hopped in the car and headed out on the road for Las Vegas, Nevada. Tony knew that this was going to be a big deal for his uncle. If it wasn't there would be no point in finishing it out. This job had to be an important one if it meant the death of his two parents. The Vegas job would've been the one to get his parents out of this lifestyle. Instead it just got them out of this life.

Tony put his bag in the trunk of the car, and then realized there was nothing inside of the trunk. "Where is everything?" he asked his uncle.

"Get in. We'll talk on the road."

As they got to driving his uncle started telling him a few things about the trip, "The car is lined. There's nothing in here with us, because no matter who's driving where, there's a chance that you can get pulled over. Of course you wouldn't have blocks of cocaine sitting in your trunk, or out in the open back seat of your car."

"I still don't understand where it all is."

"Damn, you really didn't know about any of this shit, did you?"

"Hell no! I thought we already got past that."

"I'm just messin with you. We had a pact, your dad and I, that no one would know what was going on but the two of us. Then he died so I had to drag someone else in on this."

"Thanks, remind me again where the stuff is, so I don't go opening a door and letting an ass load of crack come falling out."

"I already told you, it's lined. The whole car. Underneath the interior are bags of cocaine. The roof is padded with it. Even when you take some of the plastic siding off the interior, there's some stashed there."

"Isn't it going to be a little suspicious when we're in someone's driveway and we're pulling packs of cocaine out of the ceiling?"

"The car isn't coming back with us. We're leaving it there."

"How the hell do we get back home?"

"We fly."

The two made their way to Vegas. After a day of driving, they stopped in Kansas. They had swapped driving off and on so that they would be able to make it this far without pulling over for rest. A job had to be finished and they had very little time for sleeping. When they finally dragged themselves into their motel room it was around nine. They hadn't been in the room twenty minutes before they heard a knock on the door. Since Uncle Denny was in the bathroom, Tony answered it.

"Hi, can I help you?" he asked the man cautiously.

"I'm looking for Denny."

Denny walked out of the bathroom and dashed over to the door, "What they hell are you doing here?" He peered outside the door and pulled the young guy inside. "How the fuck did you know I was here?"

"Sorry, Denny, Blue knew that you were driving down. Thought I should follow you to make sure you don't get off track." He began to get twitchy, "So, ah, where's the stuff?"

Denny eyeballed him for a second, "What do you mean, 'where's the stuff'? You know good and damn well how it works."

"Refresh me. I must've forgot," he said as he inched towards Tony's uncle.

"What the hell is wrong with you?" Denny grabbed the guys shirt as he inched towards him. He could feel the ridge of the wire underneath his clothing, "Are you wearing a damned wire? Shit." He took his pistol out from behind his belt and shot the man without hesitation. Tony grew pale as he watched, "Tony, grab the damn bag and lets go. The cops'll be here any second."

The two raced out the door and drove quickly off into the night. Just as they were driving off they could hear the sirens in the distance. Fortunately they had already turned down a few back roads and would be out of the line of sight of the police cars. Tony sat in the passenger seat, stunned.

"What the hell is going on?" he asked his uncle. "Why would someone you work with be in connection with the cops?"

"He was Blue's second hand man. Blue didn't have shit to do with it. The cops were catching on our asses. Not yours and mine, but mine and your dad's," Denny looked over towards Tony. "He knew we were headed out there, but the cops were probably leading in on Blue and offered him some cash for information. Of course he'd never rat out his own boss, but why not rat out the competition, even if they were about to hand over their reins." Tony remained quiet and Denny continued, "There's something you should know about your dad and me. When I got him into the whole ring of things, he became the golden boy in the eyes of some of the hardest bad asses in the cartel. They took a liking to him and when our boss passed on without any children, your dad took his spot."

"Then who the hell is Blue?"

"Blue is a guy who's just as big in Vegas, as your dad was in the industry in New York. Same level of business, we're taking this stuff to Blue, to hand off our end to him. It was somewhat of a deal that would allow Blue to monopolize the cartel, but get our hands out of it. Your dad was tired of the business."

"Why would the guy you shot be in connection with the cops?"

"My guess is the cops tracked down Blue's guy, in hopes that they'd get some connection with us. It would stop us, and stop Blue from gaining territory. He probably would've gotten time taken off of a sentence. Blue's gonna have to pass us of more for that shit though."

"Then we're home free, right?"

"Damn straight."

They drove non stop, switching off the driving to make sure they would get out of the vicinity of cops following them. Finally they made their way inside the state of Nevada. Another hour and a half and they'd be handing off some of the best cocaine to the hands of a mid-west drug lord. Along with it they'd be handing off the reins of the east coast as well. Driving past the Vegas strip, they drove down secluded roads until they found themselves at a large iron gate with a speakerphone.

"Listen Tony," said Denny, "These guys are hard-asses. You haven't had any issues keeping your mouth shut so far, but don't let it start flapping now."

"Trust me, you'll have no problem with me."

"Good. Now, here's how shit's gonna go," he started to open his mouth but then a voice came over the intercom.

"Why the hell are you sitting in the car outside of my gate?" asked a demanding voice.

"Sorry, I was about to press the button," answered Denny, quickly.

"Forget about it, I'm opening the gate for you. When you drive in, park the car with James. He'll take you from there."

"Sure thing," said Denny as he rolled the window up.

"Why does he sound like he's your boss?" asked Tony.

"Because we're handing over our work to him. From here on out, this is his work, not ours."

They drove the car inside the gate, and went on the narrow winding driveway to the other side of a large barren hill. When they reached the other side they could tell that it wasn't a hill, but a garage built into the ground. The hill was a simple cover up. As they pulled closer to the garage, they saw James. As they pulled up to him, he gestured his hand out for the keys. The two parked the car, and exited it along with their bag.

"What's in the bag?" the tall man of at least three hundred pounds asked.

"A sample and some clothes," Denny said

"Give me your gun," James told him.

"What the hell?"

"Just give it to me, that way we can make sure no shit goes down."

Denny tossed him the gun and the three of them hoped into a golf cart and drove into the garage. Once they were inside James pressed a button on a remote and a large elevator door opened. He drove the golf cart into the elevator and waited for the doors to shut before pressing the down button. Once they had made their way down into the bottom floor of the elevator, the doors opened and James drove the golf cart out and up a narrow easement to a house. It was an underground tunnel of sorts, that led to what looked like a barricade.

"Where the hell are we?" said Tony, bewildered at the underground scenery.

"Who's the kid?" James asked Denny.

"My nephew. Dad was killed a day or two ago," Denny told him.

"Gotcha." James looked back at Tony, almost sympathetic. "It's an underground cavern. There's tons of em here in Nevada. Blue needed one to keep shit from nosy eyes."

"Smart move, I doubt anyone would ever find this place. It's off the radar."

Denny stared at the boy, "Stop your jabbering."

"Nothing wrong with a little small talk," said James, "I bet Blue would take a liking to the boy."

Tony felt a bit of an ego boost, before realizing who it was that would be taking a liking to him. Of course it's always nice to be complemented, but not necessarily the best complement to know that a drug overlord would have favoritism toward you. This wasn't the life for him, and he could never fathom the idea of having to walk in his fathers footsteps. Especially if the shoes to be filled were ones that could bring danger at some point or another.

The golf cart finally made it's way to an iron door. Beside the door was a button with an intercom, similar to the one that was on the outside of the gate. James exited the golf cart and pressed the button near the intercom. When the same voice came over the speaker James pressed his head to the wall and looked back at the golf cart, before waving the two over.

"Time to go up," said James.

Denny looked at Tony and gestured for him to go first. They walked through the door and around a hallway before entering a cherry stained wood paneled room. Inside the room were lush furnishings with gold embroidery. Tony could tell that, although this place could easily have been designed by a wealthy attorney, that because of the tackiness of some of the items, such as the oversized white Bengal rug, that this was either the home of a pimp or a drug handler. In this case, it was the abode of a dealer, who was about to extend his territory of work to nearly two thirds of the United States.

James led the two to sit down on a brown leather couch. Beside it was another brown sofa, somewhat smaller in size, with an older man sitting in it. He had to be in his seventies, though he looked healthy for his age. Tony was fairly surprised that the man who could run a chill down anyone's spine, was aged to the point where a lean in the wrong direction could cripple his spine.

"I'm older than you thought, aren't I?" Blue asked Tony.

"A little."

Blue smirked and lifted his eyebrow as Denny shot his nephew a dirty look.

"Oh, don't worry Denny. I like him," Blue said as he finished off his tumbler of scotch. "You're a Dinito, aren't you?"

"Ah, yes sir, I am."

"Where's your father?"

"How do you know…"

"You're his spitting image. Why are you here in his place?"

"Blue, someone came into their house a few days ago. Both of them are gone," Denny said.

"Shit."

"Someone got pissed they didn't get to dip their hands in our business." Denny stared at Blue for a minute before continuing, "Well, this ends it for our holding of the reins in our territory, it's all yours."

"Thank you. For handing it off to me. I know there were other prospective's." His mind rambled for a minute, "You did get what I asked you for, right?"

Denny nodded, and tossed him a sample.

"I can't sample the shit."

"I guarantee you, it's not crap. It's good. Not even good, it's the best shit you'll get."

"I haven't laid my hand on any of that mess in years. How I stayed in such good shape. I don't use what I sell. That's the number one rule in handling. You should know better. No wonder your brother handled the majority of everything. I'm surprised you didn't drown yourselves on the east coast."

"There's enough for seven lines though?"

"Don't waste the goods then. James, come here," said Blue as he gestured for James to walk over. "I need you to try this stuff. Make sure it's all Denny says it's cracked up to be, if I'm going to give him some additional money on top of what I'm buying him out for."

"No problem, boss," said James as his eyes lit up like a kid in a candy store.

"Not too much though, I need you to be functional to show these two to the door," James stared at Blue and he nodded, "Just one line. You can finish off your goods Denny. Then I don't want you touching the shit. Why I care so much is beyond me, but you have another family to take care of. You can't spend your life snorting when you not only have your family depending on you, but your brother's family as well. So enjoy your last hay day. I'm sure Tony will have no problem finding you two a hotel room for a night or two before driving back to New York."

Tony shook his head, "No, that's fine." He was still dealing with the shock from the death of his parents and finding out what his dad really did for a living. On top of that he was having to deal with the death of a middle man being shot by his uncle. Having to watch his uncle snort cocaine was just the icing on the cake. Wasn't too surprising for him to have another factor added in on the weirdness.

Denny took the baggy of white powdered substance from his book bag. He went to a nearby table and gently let it slide out of the bag. After he had used a razor to separate the lines, he looked to James to join him. There were seven lines, all about an inch in length. James went first, came up, and nodded to his boss about the strength of the drug.

"Enjoy this one, Denny. It's your last," said Blue.

Denny hit each of the six lines that were left after James. By the time he came up from the sixth hit he gasped deeply. Tony looked at Blue as Blue stared wide eyed at James. Blood started rushing out of Denny's nostrils, until he laid there without movement.

"He said it was strong," James said to Blue.

"What's going on, is this normal?" Tony asked, unaware of what had happened since he'd never had a run in with cocaine.

Blue felt gained leaden shoulders as he opened his mouth to speak to Tony. "Your uncle just O. D.ed"

"What the hell?" Tony exclaimed as he jumped up to rush over to his uncle's side. By the time he reached him it was too late. It took six lines of cocaine to kill Denny.

Seven

It was winter in Alaska. This year's season of bitterness had proven itself to be unusually brutal. In a small, one roomed cabin in the wilderness lived the Dowd's. Their home was about thirty miles from the nearest hospital and from this distance, there were no roads that they could take. The two had to use their plane to travel in to town, which wasn't uncommon for living out in the rural areas of Alaska. The couple had been married for fifteen years and had been trying to conceive a child from the minute they were wed. After a few years of being unable to have children, they decided to try to do infertility treatments. Thousands of dollars were spent trying to get pregnant. Not only were they paying for the infertility treatments themselves, but they were also spending money on fuel to fly to and from the nearest hospital.

Finally, after years of infertility treatments, and having many doctors tell them they shouldn't get their hopes up, they conceived a baby girl. Kerry and Jane Dowd spent their days and nights talking about the baby that they would welcome with open arms into their home. They had dreamed of this point in their life since they had met each other. Having a family was important to both of them. They had both grown up in large families of their own, and always dreamed of having hundreds of filthy diapers to change. When Jane was seven months along, she began having contractions. Kerry flew her to the nearest hospital and the doctors put her on bed rest. She began having many complications along with her contractions, even though she was following the doctors orders. At the eight month check up her doctors did an ultra sound and realized that her amniotic sac, which contained vital nutrients to their daughter, may have been leaking, thus not providing the baby what it needed to survive the entire pregnancy. The doctors ordered an immediate c-section and warned her of what a high risk she had become. Ever since the couple became pregnant, they were aware of the risks. Since Jane had such trouble conceiving, it meant that there were even greater risks that could result from her being pregnant. Also, as women age there becomes a greatened risk for not only the baby to have a birth defect, but it also increases risks for the mother, such as blood clotting. Just before the doctors removed the baby from her uterus, Jane's vitals began rapidly declining.

"Faster!" the surgeons would shout, as everyone began to scamper to their feet. Once the baby was born, they handed the her off to neo-natal nurses, to get the new baby girl ready for the world. The doctors quickly stitched up Jane as they tried their best to get her vitals up. When she began coding they did everything they could to try to keep her alive, including resuscitation. All of their efforts to save the new mother were in vain. Jane Dowd had died during childbirth.

Of course, at first Kerry had trouble knowing what to do to raise a little girl all on his own. He and his wife had struggled for year to have a child, and now that they had one, Jane had died. Three years down the road Kerry met a widow who's husband had died in a mining accident in north Alaska. She was left alone to deal with four rambunctious boys, all of whom were at least three years older than Janie. The two halves of a whole family came together to create their own, oversized Alaskan family. A new home was built that would fit four sons, a daughter, and two parents. They still lived on the outskirts of the city, but had no need for plane trips into town.

Growing up with a family of men had man pros and cons for Janie. She grew up learning the fundamentals of nature. Although her dad would take the boys hunting, she got to go on all the trips with the boys, as well as many daddy/daughter hunting trips. She could shoot any moose dead with a rifle or a bow and arrow. In addition to hunting and fishing, she gained insight on what it really meant to be a man. Many women lean on the mother figures they have, but it was extremely important in Janie's life to understand the importance of a male figure, and how they should act.

One evening nearing the end of a high school date, Janie was staring out at the open stars with the boy that she'd been crushing on for years. "The stars really are beautiful out here," she told him.

"Not nearly as beautiful as you are," he said as he leaned in to kiss her. The two made out for a good twenty minutes before things started heating up. Her date began putting his arm up his shirt when she pushed him off of her.

"What the hell are you doing?"

"What people usually do when they're about to have sex."

"Sex? Are you kidding me? This is the first date I've ever been on with you."

"So what? Most girls don't even need a date to put out."

"We're in high school. The only people who might even consider putting out on the first date are party crazy girls in their twenties, and even then it's usually whores who do it."

"People said you were cool as shit. They were wrong though," he looked at her disgusted. "To think I wasted a Saturday night with you."

"Look asshole, you may be somewhat easy to look at, but you're no Greek God. If anyone wasted their Saturday night here, it was me. I could've been out hunting with my brothers but decided to go out with your douche ass."

"I'm taking you home."

"No, shit you're taking me home. When you do, you better make sure to leave me the hell alone."

As they pulled up into the driveway of her house he said, "I guess I shouldn't linger too long, your daddy may come out and try and shoot me when you tattle on me."

"Honey," Janie said, staring the guy between the eyes with a sweet yet sinister smile on her face, "you don't have to worry about my daddy."

"Smart move, for a prude."

"Listen dumbass. You won't have to worry about my daddy because I'll shoot you myself. If I even hear of you treating another girl like you just treated me, I'll come hunt you down and have your head on my wall as a trophy." Janie slammed the door and leaned in on the rolled down window, "You have thirty seconds from the minute I run inside to make yourself disappear. I'll be back with my shotgun if you're still here." She took off inside as the boy burned rubber trying to leave her driveway as fast as possible.

It was expected that the guys she ran into would treat her with respect, and since many boys growing up are anything but mature, she often didn't have too much patience for them. Even if she did have the rare male courting her, her brothers would be on the up and up. If anyone ever broke her heart, or tried doing something stupid, they would have four big tall burly brothers to deal with.

When Janie grew up she bought herself a cabin in the woods. Her livelihood was based around hunting. She was a hunter by trade, and it put dinner on the table in many ways than just one. Competitions were where she made the most of her money, and she would often hunt game and sell it to local butchers. She was a tiny woman, with the gumption of ten body builders, but she didn't have near enough room in her body to eat the amount of meat that she hunted on a daily basis. Her living was built upon the fundamentals that her dad gave her. For her to be able to do what she loved for a living was all that she could ask for. Being able to be out in the wilderness alone, without having to deal with any man, made her proud. It was nice to have the comfort of knowing she didn't need to rely on anyone.

She had made a name for herself among the hunting community and it paid off well. Not only was she a phenomenal hunter, but she was a good looking one too. After winning her first national moose hunting competition, she was given contracts by many of the leading hunting outfitters to be a spokesperson and model. Her step-mother taught her many natural beauty recipes, which gave her porcelain skin, bright white teeth, and shiny long brown hair. Fortunately for her, there wasn't much competition as a female hunter. She had a few rivals, but none could out hunt her. She had been trained by her father, who in his own right was one of a kind himself. Making a way for herself in the hunting world made it easier for her in ways, but more difficult in others. She knew that even though she was a well respected hunter, there would always be people looking down on her for simply being a girl. There was nothing she could do about the issue that many people would have against her. It was simply how she was born.

Although there were a lot of hunters who respected her in the field, there were the rare few that she would come across that would stick up their nose in her direction. On a few occasions, she would be on a hunting trip and some ignorant hunter would remark to the entry sheet, 'Oh you have a girl here'. When it would come time to hunting she would wipe the floor with them, and they'd usually complain. They wouldn't be complaining about their own crappy hunting skills, but rather the fact that they allowed a girl in the competition. On one of the competitions she hunted in, there were actually a group of men who put together a petition asking for the committee running the competition to have a female contest for her and other women to compete in. Of course they were denied, not only because Janie was the only woman competing, but also because it was only their names on the petition, as no one else was interested in being so sexist. She was easily titled the best female hunter, and many would justify that she was the best hunter period, regardless of gender.

There was a bar in town that Janie would venture to often after a day of hunting. It was located in a little hole in the wall between the butcher shop she'd take her meat to, and a nail salon. Occasionally she would joke that more of the customers were buzzed off of the fumes from next door, rather than the beers they'd had. It wasn't necessarily the nicest bar in town, but it was her bar. She knew that when she walked through the doors of the bar that she was home. At twenty six, Janie had been visiting this bar for ten years. Of course, she had been coming in to soak up the environment when she was underage. Her eldest brother would work the bar and let Janie sneak in when it was his night to work. She wasn't drinking until she was legally able to drink, but she just loved the way she felt when she was at the bar. The wood paneling reminded her of being outdoors and the stale cigarette smoke drifting through the room reminded her the steam coming off of the hot springs as it meets the bitter winter air. It was like a home away from home for her. She could sit in the corner and read if she wanted to and no one would even care. Coming from a small town had it's perks that way.

One evening, after a long day of hunting, Janie stopped by the bar for a drink. Her hair had been matted up from keeping it under a cap, and she hadn't bothered putting any makeup on, for fear it would get messed up anyway and having been a waste of time. Even though she looked rough, she was still gorgeous with sweat stains galore. She loved the way it felt as she walked through the door and heard the door chime. It was even nicer to hear a familiar bartender shout out their warm hello in her direction.

"Janie!" shouted her favorite bartender. He was a good looking guy in his early thirties and had been working bar here ever since her brother worked there. Not only was he a regular bartender, but he was also a co-owner of the place. A few years back his dad had decided to let him on board with the ownership, since he'd taken such a liking for the place.

"Hey Chuck!" said Janie as she walked through the threshold of the bar. She hung her wool jacket and cap up on one of the coat hangers on the wall and made her way toward her favorite stool at the bar.

"How's the day been? Anything good?" he asked her.

"Great, actually. Got a couple geese and an elk."

"Pay day for Janie," he said with a wink.

She began blushing before she could even think of anything to say to him. "I guess you could say so."

A burly man with a lot of facial hair came from the bathroom and sat down beside Janie and took a swig from his beer. Chuck brought Janie a lager and the man chuckled and said, "You really think you can handle that beer, little girl?"

"Excuse me?" Janie said heated.

"Never seen a little girl like you try and drink a beer like that," he waved Chuck over as he grabbed his gut, laughing, "You may want to get a barf bag ready for this one."

"Look asshole, I can drink any beer and hold my own far better than you." She looked the man up and down and continued, "And as for me, I actually get up off my ass now and then so my beer doesn't give me a spare tire."

"Oh, she's feisty to."

Janie reared her arm back and slammed a punch in his left eye. "Watch who you mess with ass-wipe."

The man looked around the bar stunned, as everyone laughed, including the bartenders. "Are you not going to do anything? Call the police!"

"Listen, mister," Chuck came over and said, "I'm not sure who you are, but this is the first time I've seen your face around here. Rather than trying to mess with the locals, you should keep your judgments to yourself. Miss Dowd was standing her ground and you wouldn't leave her alone. I think she just showed you who the little girl is around here."

"I don't need this shit. I have my own goodies at the room that I got from a buddy down in Vegas. I like a beer, but a good line or two never hurt anyone. If you're OK with letting a girl get away with murder on a double standard then you don't need my business."

"Everyone, especially including Janie, wouldn't mind you taking your business back to your room," Chuck said.

The man pieced the two names together, "Janie Dowd?" the man said looking from the bartender to the tiny girl sitting beside him. "You mean, Janie Dowd the hunter?" He started chuckling again.

"Do I need to make your right eye match the left?" Janie asked the man.

"No, I'm sorry, I just think it's hilarious that I just got sucker punched by the best female hunter in history."

Janie looked into her beer glass and up at him, "Best hunter period," she said with a tilt of her glass as she eyed Chuck.

"Well, you may be a pretty damn good hunter, but I wouldn't say the best hunter ever."

"Oh really, and who would you say is?"

"Not sure there barbie, but even though you're good, you could never be as good as a man."

Chuck jumped over the bar just in time for Janie's blow to land on his face, instead of the face of the new bar patron. "Janie, you need to cool down," said Chuck

"Yeah, you may want to watch it missy, I wouldn't want you having a law suit on your hands."

"Get this asshole, instead of a lawsuit, why don't we just settle this 'man enough' shit on our own. You and me."

"Do you really expect me to fight a girl?"

"No, not a fight exactly."

"Oh, you want me to compete against you? Like a hunt off?"

Janie nodded her head, "Yes, exactly. A hunt off."

The man sat and thought for a minute, he wasn't sure if a hunt off with one of the best hunters in America was the best idea, especially since he wasn't some big name hunter. He shrugged, "Sure why not, nothing to loose, lots to prove."

"And what's that?" asked Janie.

"That even though you may be the best hunter when it comes to females, even a hunter like myself could whoop your ass, just because I'm a man." Right then he leaned back as she took a swing. "Saw it coming," he said and winked. The man paid his tab and stood up from the bar.

"Tomorrow's Friday, and my availability is wide open. Tomorrow, we hunt. Biggest elk wins."

"Of course," Janie said nodding. "After all, size does matter," she said holding up her pinkie finger, wearing a frown and staring in the direction of his private parts.

The man sneered at her and left the bar. The other patrons at the bar shouted their hoorays that the man had finally left. After being a regular at the bar for a good ten years, Janie had gained a group of fans. Many of them knew how great a hunter she was. They loved the fact that a girl from their own home town had made a name for herself. Not only had she made a name for herself, but she'd also made a name for her town. Her name and hometown were side by side in many magazines. Although it didn't necessarily bring too much tourism to the town, she was a well known hunter after all, not a movie star, it did bring hunting tournaments. The hunting tournaments helped the economy of the small town greatly. Whenever the competitions would come to town they would house hunters in the nearby lodges. Restaurants would see greater profits at the end of the day during tournament weeks. The people of this small town felt gratitude towards little Janie. They would always be on her side.

The next morning she went to the bar to wait on her competition. She wanted to have the upper ground, so she arrived early. She got to the bar at five the next morning. Even though the bar closed at three in the morning on weekdays, Chuck was beyond willing to help out his long time friend have a head up on the competition. Around five forty five, the overweight man came into the bar, ready to go out for a hunt.

"Nice of you to join us, asshole," said Janie.

"I thought we'd agreed on six?" the man asked.

"Six as a start time. Lets go, I'm ready to beat your ass."

"I wanted to apologize before we set out on our adventure."

Janie looked the man up and down, "Hah, you do realize that if you don't hunt, you lose by default."

"Precisely, and I thought that I'd offer up my apologies, because I am going to hunt so much better than you, and make you look like an idiot in your home town."

"Good luck with that."

Chuck got in between the two of them, "Alright you two, shake hands before trekking off. Go whichever way you want, and be back with something by seven tonight with some game."

The hunters extended their hands, and shook on it. The man squinted his eyes at Janie and said, "May the best man win."

Janie squeezed his hand tightly and he began to wince, "She. Will."

They left the bar and headed out on their own. She watched the man go off into the direction of the south woods. Luckily for her, she knew this town like the back of her hand. She knew that the direction he was headed in didn't have many large animals, mainly deer and rabbits nestled in those woods. He'd be lucky if he made it back to the bar with buck. Fortunately, she was going to head off to the woods where she and her father hunted as a little girl. Her dad had taught her everything she needed to know about hunting. In this land she even knew the patterns of the animals. They would shift throughout the day and week. She was so good at reading the pattern of the local animals, that it was as though she could smell which direction a moose was running in. She would have this hunt won easily.

She had her rifle on her back, along with extra rounds of bullets in her pocket. Although she was a straight-shooter, and a damn good one, she wanted to make sure she had all she would need to beat the arrogant asshole from the bar. It often would only take her one shot to land her a large elk, but she had to be sure. She was going to hunt the entire day. If she had a hit by noon, she would continue hunting. She brought along a map in her pocket so she could mark where her kills were and how large they were. Then when she'd shot all that she had time to shoot, she'd refer to the map and go back and get whichever animal was the largest. After going back to the bar to show her winnings, she'd take her truck to go collect up her earnings for the day. It would be a day of hunting for the sake of winning, and would give her a little money in her pocket from the butcher as well.

It was a foggy day, caught in between the times of full sun and full darkness. The wandering hunter had dragged his feet to her hometown bar at the perfect time of year. She still had enough dusk to be able to sneak around some creatures, but enough daylight to be able to see them while camouflaged. She had the benefit either way. Although the sun would be going down around five, she'd still be able to have enough daylight to hunt and drive her truck to get her meat without having to worry about any nighttime dangers. Out in the woods of Alaska there were many dangers that hunters would have to deal with. Having bad footing could lead you down a hill with a sprained ankle, be caught in the wrong area of the woods in the dark could lead you straight into the path of wild animals.

Janie parked her car along the side of a quiet road way and made her journey into the deep woods. She walked on for a good thirty minutes before finding one of her favorite spots to hunt. She climbed up the tree and sat in her tree stand and waited for something to come by. An hour had drifted by when she heard something rustling through the trees. Grabbing her binoculars, she peered out through the distance. It was a big one. She quickly, yet quietly grabbed her rifle and shot the elk. She climbed out of the tree to make sure that she'd actually killed it. Upon inspection she found it laying there, dead, no suffering. She got beside the elk and began praying for it. This was a ritual that Janie had with the animals that she killed. It was always a sad moment when she killed an animal. Most people would assume that hunters are heartless people who could care less about animals. Janie wasn't one of those hunters. She prayed for every animal she shot, that their lives weren't lost in vain and that they would be of some use to someone. It would break her heart when she'd stumble upon an animal she shot, only to find it still alive but in writhing in extreme pain and suffering.

Janie marked this one on her map and made her way through the woods. She realized that it probably wasn't the best idea to leave her kills laying around, when there was another hunter competing against her. Especially not a conniving one who would probably try to take one of her animals and claim it as his own. Rather than going further away, as she'd planned, she stayed in the vicinity of two miles. There were many elk for her to find in these woods anyway. In the area that the man was hunting, he would be lucky to find one elk. That alone could get him wandering in other directions, which she was worried about to an extent. When she began thinking about the other hunter, she reeled in her focus back on herself and her hunt. There was nothing for her to be worried about.

It was already around five, and she knew she would have to start wrapping things up in the woods, if she was going to make it back in time. Checking her map, she realized she'd shot a large, probably eight hundred pound, elk earlier in the day. This was her biggest kill, so she should get back to where it was when she shot it. Making her way back, she couldn't help but be proud of her kills for the day. She'd shot 3 elk, and a rabbit. All of which she'd sell to the butcher later that evening after having her brothers help collect the carcasses. She felt an uneasy gut feeling as she made her way back to the spot where her biggest kill was. It was hunter's instinct, but she didn't know why.

As she made her way over a small hill she looked where her elk had laid and realized what her uneasy feeling was about. There, feasting on her best kill were a pack of wolves, blood and guts dripping from the fur around their mouth. "Shit", she thought to herself as she pulled the riffle off of her shoulders and around in front of her. Just as she was pulling the riffle down, one of the wolves looked up at her and started growling. She shot one, but it hit him in the hip, rather than the heart, and he screamed. He along with the six other wolves came running in her direction. She was screwed.

It was eight o'clock back at the town bar. The other hunter was there with his prize, a deer. "Well I guess I win by forfeit. I guess that girl just didn't have it in her. Couldn't get a kill other than some mongoose, and was too ashamed to show back up here."

"That's not like Janie, though," said Chuck, "something happened."

"Oh, sure, take up for your hometown hero."

"Look," Chuck said leaning in towards the man's face, "I can tell that you're an asshole, but something's not right here. A hunter who wins hundreds of awards and is a spokesperson doesn't just 'not show up'."

The man saw the worry in the bartender's eyes, "Shit, I guess you're right."

The bartenders and patrons got in their trucks and headed out to their cars.

"Where do you think she went?" Chuck asked her brother.

"The north woods. It's the best dwelling for elk," he said.

The trucks took off speeding towards the woods. It was pitch black by then, and they all were suited up with flashlights, and riffles of their own. Chuck was wondering in a path over a hill. He got to the top of the hill and saw what he thought was a dead elk. Getting closer, he realized it had been torn apart by wolves. As he kept walking he saw a body, and it hit him. They were too late, Jannie had been attacked, and ripped apart by seven wolves. A whole pack of them.

Eight

Elle Lockwood always dreamed of making the world a better place. As a child she would dress up and pretend to have numerous occupations. One day she'd have her stuffed animals sitting in the kitchen as she took their meal orders. The next day she'd have her dolls laid out on her bed as she performed operations on their little bodies. The role playing game she took part in most often was that of being a teacher. She would line her dolls up equal distance around her room and she'd lay a paper out in front of each one of them. Then she'd go in front of all of her stuffed animals and draw on a miniature art easel. Playing teacher could go on for hours, while her other games would last a good half hour at most.

When it came down to deciding what she would study in college, she knew that she would have to study to become a teacher. The yester years of when she would play teacher with her stuffed animals had been engrained in her mind. Even as she progressed through middle school and high school she would always play the role of the leader. It was a given that no matter what club she was in, or what circle of friends she had, everyone knew that she would be leading the group in one way or the other. Elle studied hard, and made sure that she got into one of the best universities in the state. Given that she was going for a teaching degree, she wanted to ensure that she had the best scores and grades possible. Teaching had many benefits, so it meant that many people would opt for the career. It was also a fairly solid job, at least when she had began studying in college it was. Even then, she wanted to make sure that she had the highest grade point average possible, so that she would be able to teach at the school of her choice. While many people may major in education, the one's with lower GPA's usually ended up working in less appealing positions on rougher sides of town.

When Elle graduated college she not only graduated with honors, but as valedictorian of her graduating class. Many slots in the teaching field were opening up and she had a lot of inquiries from schools in her area. She had grown up in a wealthy family in a nice part of New Hampshire, and she couldn't have imagined ever living any where else. Her location was perfect in her eyes. Although many of her friends spread their wings after high school to venture off far and wide for colleges around the country, many of them were finding their ways back home. This would mean that she could still live in the same small town she grew up in, and have friends that she had cherished her whole life. She decided to work in a fairly expensive private school that was located about thirty minutes from her house. It was close enough that she didn't have to worry too much about gas and traffic, but it was far enough that she wouldn't have to worry about running in to her student's parents or co-workers after hours. She believed that the key to success in life was having a distinct division between work and home life. Elle was a firm believer in not taking work home with her.

During Elle's second year teaching at the private school she worked at, she was assigned to an after school program. The faculty had been wanting to create a leadership program for the older students to participate in, but hadn't had any teachers come forward that were interested in chaperoning the club. After Elle's first year at the school, her colleagues realized how much dedication she had for her students. They asked her if she would be willing to take part in the leading of the club and she cheerfully joined on. At that point in time she was a single young woman with very few responsibilities other than her job.

In October a faculty member moved across the country to follow her military husband. After a few substitute teachers had passed through the fourth grade classroom, they finally were able to gain a new full time teacher. His name was Derrick Shafer, and he was fresh out of an Ivy League college where he gained a Masters degree in Education. Since teaching jobs had been fleeting, he had been sitting by the wayside for the past summer, searching for jobs to no avail. Once he teamed up with the private school, they soon found out that he had many similarities to Miss Lockwood, and that he would be a wonderful addition to the leadership club. One day after school he walked into a club meeting for the first time.

Leaning on the doorway, he tapped on the threshold, "Knock, knock."

Elle, surprised, turned to the handsome man standing in the doorway. She hadn't gotten a chance to introduce herself to the new teacher, but had seen him in the hallway a time or two. "Oh, hi," she mustered up the courage to say. The students were working diligently on posters to hang up for the next pep rally, so she walked over to him without disturbing the kids.

"I hope I'm not bothering you," said Derrick.

"Of course not," she blushed sheepishly.

"I'm Mr. Shafer, you can call me Derrick," he said with an extended hand.

Elle reached down and shook his hand, "I'm Miss Lockwood. Elle Lockwood. You must be the new fourth grade teacher."

"Yes, I am. So, I hear this is some club you have here," he said looking at all the students working.

"It is, indeed. They're wonderful students. Each of them are on some sort of sports team, or are involved in choir or drama. All of them the creme of the crop for their groups. Presidents, treasurers. Those sorts."

"Ah, so it's a true blue leadership club," he said walking into the classroom.

"Yes, but none of them are forced to be here, they all joined at their own interest. Not all of them are on the board of their other clubs, but they all are in some sort of extra-curricular activity other than this one."

"I see. So, tell me, what exactly do they do? For leadership work that is, other than being involved in other clubs amongst the student body."

"Well, the student's and myself go out into the community and help those in need. Currently we've gone out and cleaned two neighborhood parks in the rougher sides of town that needed a sprucing up. Each of the students have paired up with a 'grandmother, or grandfather' from different nursing homes around the area, who they take care of in some way, shape or form. Usually it's to just keep them company, but once a month we get them all together for a luncheon, so that they can meet other kids, as well as other elders in their community."

"That sounds very endearing," Derrick said as he leaned closer in towards Elle. "I have a shelter I used to help in the soup kitchen at. During Christmas they would give me a list of families in need, and since I grew up with well to do parents, we would go out and create a Christmas for them, that they otherwise wouldn't have been able to afford. If you'd like, and if your students would be interested, we could group them up to go out this Christmas to the different families as their Santas."

"They'd love that, I'm sure." Elle stared at his dark blue eyes and hesitated, "You don't think that you'd be interested in helping me run the club, would you? I mean it's not much to run, the kids take care of things well themselves, but it's good for the heart to see the kids doing great things for the world they live in."

"I'd love to help out. Some of the faculty had actually mentioned that I should try to team up with you, but I thought I'd come out and see how things were myself." He caught himself staring at Elle too closely, "The club I mean, of course."

"Of course."

That was the beginning of Derrick and Elle. They spend that whole year enjoying one another's company in the classroom, as well as outside of the classroom. There were many parallels to their lifestyles and the families they came from. Both were clean cut teachers, and both of them went to prestigious colleges that gave them solid footing for a private school career. During the summer of the next year Derrick took Elle to a creek for a picnic.

"This is beautiful, Derrick."

"I thought you'd like it." Derrick began unpacking the crescent sandwich's he'd made earlier in the day, and set them out in front of him and Elle. He reached back into the basket and winked at Elle, "How would you like," he grabbed two wine glasses, "a glass of wine? Your favorite."

"Aren't you charming," she said as her eyes lit up. They had taken a drive around the countryside and were finally putting a warm ending on a beautiful summers day. "I would love a glass."

As they sipped their first taste of the wine, Derrick remembered something, "Ah, I have something else for you. It's in the car though, I hope you don't mind if I run back and get it."

"No, that's fine."

After he'd made his way to the car and back to the blanket where his girlfriend was nestled, he laid down beside her with his head in his hand. "Elle," he said as he pulled his other hand in between them, "I want to spend the rest of my life with you. Would you be my wife?"

"Yes!" she squealed and they kissed, tasting of wine that they had just shared.

One could say that the years they grew together were some of the best years they had. Shortly after they got married the couple became pregnant with a little girl. Once Elle was eight months along, she went on maternity leave. She remained on leave for three months before talking with Derrick about going back to work. Though they had decided that it wasn't too soon, Elle had second thoughts. After a long night of pillow talk, Elle realized that she wanted to stay home with her daughter, at least until Lula was old enough to go to school. Of course they would have been able to get their daughter into a day care program easily, Elle simply couldn't stand the thought of leaving their baby in the hands of someone else. Especially given the horror stories she'd read online about things that happen in day cares.

Although the Shafer's had a great love for one another, they quickly let the responsibility of keeping up with their relationship slip to the side. It was hard keeping a flame lit between the two when there were diapers to be changed at all times of the night. Of course, since Derrick worked full time and Elle was a stay at home mom, she would get up in the middle to tend to their daughter when she would wake up in the middle of the night. This took a deep toll on Elle, she learned to sleep during the times when her daughter would sleep, and would make use of herself when she wasn't needed by her baby. She would do all of the cleaning around the house and made sure that things were spik and span for when her husband would arrive home.

As their daughter aged, the relationship between Derrick and Elle became even more fragile. One evening when Derrick got home, he fell apart. It had been a long day at school and he had planned on coming home to relax. He had told himself that tonight was the night when he'd apologize for neglecting his relationship with his wife. Derrick parked the car in the garage, grabbed his suitcase and walked up to the doorway. He walked through the hallway and his body weight shifted as he fell to the ground.

"What the hell is this!" he shouted. Derrick looked around the room at the wreck of toys strewn everywhere.

Elle ran into the room, and quickly following behind her was four year old Lula. "What happened, are you OK.?" she asked as she kneeled over at her husbands side. She reached out for his hand, but he snatched her arm away.

"Hell no I'm not OK, Elle. I'm gone ten hours a day at minimum, and you would think when I got home that I could at least come home to a clean house. I mean, seriously what the hell have you been doing all day?"

"Are you kidding me? I've been doing laundry, and mopping and cleaning all day."

"Really? Then what's with all of the clutter?"

Elle looked around and saw the toys that Lula had been playing with, "What, her toys? She had been playing. I was about to start dinner and she was already playing with her toys so I thought if she were to keep playing with them, it would keep her occupied long enough for me to start dinner."

"So wait, you haven't even started dinner?"

"I was walking to the kitchen about to, when you came in the door raising hell."

"So, let me get this straight. I've been gone all day, while you've supposedly been doing laundry and cleaning up, yet when I get home I see this house looking like a tornado swept through it, toys scattered everywhere. You haven't even made dinner yet? Seriously, Elle, what the hell do you do all day anyways? Sit in front of the TV eating chocolates?"

"You have got to be out of your mind."

"Well, I mean, look at the house, Elle." He looked her body up and down, "Look at you. Would it really surprise you that I'd think you ate candies on the couch all day?"

"Are you calling me fat now?"

"I never said you were fat, but I am saying you're not in the shape you used to be."

"You did this to me! I had your child, I'm not overweight, I work out every day, but dammit so what if I'm a size six and not a size two any more. Is that why you married me?"

"No it's not, I married you because I thought you'd make a good wife. But hell you can't even do the normal things that wife's do."

Elle placed her hands on her hips, "What, pray tell, is it that normal wife's do, Derrick?"

"They clean, for Christ's Sake! They clean and they have dinner ready on the table when their husband gets home from a long day at work."

"I do clean, I just have someone coming behind me after I clean. I was about to start cooking when you came home raising hell." Elle looked down at their daughter who had tears swelling up in her eyes, "And in front of your daughter." She picked Lula up, "You don't give a damn about either of us. You never even spend time with her."

Derrick took the hit to heart, "Yes I do. That's my baby, and I spend a lot of time with her."

"Hah! When?"

"All the time!"

"Whenever I ask you to. Even then you give me hell about it. Whenever I go to the grocery store, I practically have to beg you to let her stay with you."

"I kept her last weekend when you went, I don't see why you can't take her with you to the grocery store when you stay at home all day anyways."

"Do you understand how difficult it is taking a child to a grocery store? Not only does she reach for everything with a familiar cartoon character on it, but she freaks out when it's time to leave." She stared at her stern husband, "Do you not think that I deserve a little break now and then?"

"What do you need a break for? You stay at home all day. It's not like you actually work or do anything."

Elle let out a deep sigh, "Of course. I can't live my life like this, Derrick. I'm going to sleep on the twin bed in Lula's room tonight. I'm calling my aunt and seeing if I can stay with her for a while."

"You can't just leave. What am I going to do with Lula?"

"Don't worry Derrick, I wouldn't dream about leaving you alone with your own child. I understand you have zero clue how to take care of a four year old."

"That's not what I meant, but you can't just leave with Lula. You're my wife and she's my baby!"

"I am leaving, and she'll always be your baby, but I can't live my life like this with you. You never see anything I do. There's always something that you're looking for that I haven't accomplished. I'm tired of it."

That night Elle called in take out food and the three of them ate as a family for the last time. Derrick knew that he'd crossed the line that evening, but nothing he could do or say would change the mind of his wife. She was set on leaving. They made sure to be as calm and peaceful for the rest of the night so that their daughter wouldn't have to worry about anything. Elle was sick and tired of being treated the way that Derrick treated her, and even though he tried later that evening to say things to keep her home, she refused to forgive him. She was tired of not being enough for him. She was beyond tired of his nagging.

Elle made a phone call to her Aunt Beth. The phone rang and rang until there was an answer on the other end of the line, "Hello?"

"Hey Aunt Beth. It's Elle."

"Well, hey sweetie. What're you up to."

Elle twirled the cord between her fingers, "Oh, nothing. Just was wondering if you were busy this weekend. Thought it might be nice to see your face. I know Lula misses you."

"Of course, my doors always open. It would be nice to have you, Lula, and Derrick over for the weekend. Your Uncle Bert's up in Alaska for a hunting tournament in honor of the Dowd girl's death."

"Ah, yeah I had heard about what happened. Knew Uncle Bert had competed with her a few times."

"Yeah, he could never get a leg up on her. Said she was a real sweet heart though. Tragic."

"Definitely," Elle got back on her train of thought. "Aunt Beth, it's just going to be me and Lula this time around."

"Oh really? My favorite nephew-in-law isn't sick is he?"

"Only in the head," she could feel the confusion on the other end of the line. "We had an argument. I just need some time away."

"Well, you know my door's always open for you."

"Alright, I'm driving out tomorrow."

"Be safe, I love you," said her aunt and Elle hung up the phone and began drowning herself in tears.

No one in the family knew that they were having issues in their marriage. Often it was hard for Derrick and Elle to even see the signs that they were having issues in their marriage. They rarely spent time with one another, but half of the time that they were with one another, Derrick was complaining about something. He had grown bitter supporting the family on his own. It wasn't that he was unable to support the family, Elle wasn't a spender, it was more of the fact that he enjoyed the spunk his wife had when she was at work. She had lost the spark, and he would find anything he could pick on to say something to her. He'd become a naggy husband.

The next morning Elle put the suitcases in the trunk of her car. She walked back up to the doorsteps where her husband was standing with their daughter at his side.

"I really wish you'd stay Elle," Derrick said as he stared longingly into her eyes.

Elle broke eye contact and looked at their porch swing, "I can't. You've been too unsupportive, and I can't live the rest of my life like this. Life is meant for living, and I can't live when I'm with you."

Derrick's chest sunk, "OK," he said as he picked up his daughter and buckled her in her car seat. "Be a sweet girl for mommy, alright?" Lula nodded and he kissed her forehead, "I'll see you in a little while, sweety."

Elle buckled up and Derrick knocked on her driver side window, "I'm so sorry, Elle. I really am."

"I understand," she exhaled deeply. "I just need some time to clear my head, Derrick. I love you, you know that. This relationship just has grown so unhealthy."

"I can change for you, Elle."

"As much as I'd like that, I'm not so sure it can happen. We were so close, and like minded, but we've grown so far apart. We just need to move one baby step at a time." She looked at the clock on her dashboard, "Look, we've got a few hours of driving to do, so I need to be going."

"I understand." Derrick kissed his wife goodbye and waved as she backed down the driveway.

The two girls embarked off on their own little adventure. Even though Elle was upset at leaving her husband and her house, she was excited for the new things on the horizon. It was likely that she would be going back to her husband at some point in time, but for now she needed to clear her head. Hopefully while she was gone, he would realize how much he really needed her. She thought that he had grown ungrateful for everything she did. While she was gone, he would surely realize everything that she did for him. He would see how much cleaning she took part in, and how much cooking she did. Derrick would have it easier though, because he wouldn't have a four year old running around to keep up with. He wouldn't be able to see how much it took to take care of a young child all day. She grew tempted to take Lula back to her husband, so he could experience what it was really like to be a parent. Just as she reached for the phone, it started ringing.

She answered the phone, "Hello?"

"Hey," it was Derrick. "How close are you two from getting to your aunts house. It's been a couple hours."

"We're about thirty miles away."

"Oh, OK. Are you going straight there?"

"I'm not sure, why?" she asked, growing irritated.

"I don't know, I just was wanting to see if you guys had made it safely. I know I have a hard time showing it, but I really do love you Elle."

"I know you do Derrick."

From the backseat, Lula started crying, "Mommy!" she shouted.

"Hang on Derrick," she said as she averted her attention away from the cell phone and on to the daughter in the back seat. "What is it Lula-bug?"

"I spilled my juice."

"Dammit. Hang on honey," she held the phone up to hear ear with her shoulder as she reached for napkins.

"Is everything OK.?" Derrick asked.

"Yes, everything's fine, Lula just spilled her juice all over her. Hang on a second, k?" She reached the napkins back to Lula and she took them from her. "OK, I'm back" Elle said after she finished taking care of Lula.

"I know that I've neglected our relationship Elle. Work just became the priority. Then I started missing you, so instead of complementing you or fostering our love, I really just let things slide and used every opportunity I got a hold of to pick away at you."

"Things will work themselves out, Derrick. Even if we wont work out, things will work out, I'm sure."

"I love you Elle! Just come home, I can't live my life without you."

"Moooommmyy!!!" screamed Lula, from the backseat.

"Shit, Derrick, I have to drive, I can't handle you fussing at me and Lula fussing at me and driving all at the same time." Elle turned her attention to her daughter once again, "What is it?"

"My clothes are wet," the little girl said crying.

"Dammit, I'm going to have to pull over, Derrick. I'll call you back." Elle thought she'd hung up the phone, but she didn't click the right button and he stayed on the line. She grabbed some more napkins that were sitting next to her and turned around and handed them to her daughter. "Here baby, I'll pull over in just a minute."

When Elle turned around to fix her eyes on the road, she saw three cars wrecked in the lane right in front of her. She tried her best to slam on the brakes, but it was too late. Her car plowed into the car in front of her. Lula started screaming and when Elle reopened her eyes she fixated them to her rear-view mirror. She watched as a large eighteen wheeler slammed into her car.

Derrick heard everything that happened. He tried to call 9-1-1, but they were already on the scene. Sadly, it was too late. There had been an eight car pile up.

Nine

Jessie Lennon was on the first red-eye of her life. She'd tried to get some sleep earlier in the day, but wasn't able to drift off because of the excitement of a new town. Looking over at her dad, she could see that despite the rest of the family being asleep, he was still awake, reading one of his books as usual.

"Psst, dad." She said quietly, hoping not to wake anyone else.

"Hmm?" her dad whispered in her direction as he tipped his reading glasses to the front of his nose.

"Even though we're on a plane in the middle of the night, I'm really excited that we get to move to Florida. I was almost freaking out when it came down to Panama City and North Dakota."

"I know, we're all glad it wasn't North Dakota, but as you know home is where the military sends you." He stared at his daughter for a moment, "goodness, you're really growing up on me, girl. You should have a good time going to high school at the beach. I know I wouldn't be complaining."

"Yeah. I mean I'm sure that it'll be a lot easier making friends at the beach, where everyone is free spirited, than in was in Oklahoma where everyone grew up with one another."

"Well, it was only a year while I was overseas. You had family there. Couldn't have been too bad," he nudged her shoulder.

"Please, mom told you the story about cousin Angie, right?" Jessie's eyes darted around the plane for a quick second making sure no one was waking up from her conversation, "That girl was pure evil."

"You have to realize that sometimes girls get jealous. Especially when they've grown up knowing everyone within a ten mile radius."

"Yeah, I guess you're right."

Her dad let out a big sigh, "Get some sleep, kiddo. Tomorrow will be here sooner than you know it. I plan on you doing a good deal of unpacking too."

They both chuckled and she plugged her earphones into her MP3 player and dozed off. By the time they landed at the PCB airport it was eight a.m. Everyone on a red-eye tries their best to sleep, but often comfort is lacking in a seat that's a foot wide and reclines from a ninety degree angle to a ninety two degree angle. Regardless of how many neck pillows you have, or melatonin you take, chances are you will land in your new town drowsy and jet lagged.

"Gooooood Morning ladies and gentlemen," the airline attendant said over the intercom, "Welcome to Panama City! We hope you all enjoyed your flight and had a good nights rest." Everyone on the plane grunted at the mention of a good nights rest.

As the Lennon family, the Mr., Mrs., Jessie, and her little brother DJ, exited the airport they were hit with the humid salty air of the beach. Jessie took a big inhale, "Ahhh, I think I'm going to like it here," she said to her family.

"I'm sure you are honey," said Mrs. Lennon.

"When are we going to the beach!?" asked DJ with excitement.

"After we get into our house and do a little unpacking. The movers should be here around noon, which would give you and the kids a little time to go exploring if you want to, Sarah" said Mr. Lennon.

"Well, what do you guys think?" she asked her children.

The two children agreed that it would be a wonderful time to go explore the beach nearby. As they opened the door to their new home, they all became flushed with amazement. For base housing, this was definitely a step up from the previous homes they'd lived in. The house had a foyer that led to an open concept living room and dining room. Just off of the side of the dining room was an open kitchen with all brand new appliances. The rooms for the kids were much bigger than the ones they'd stayed in before. Even though it was a carpeted house, as most base houses are, it was brand new carpeting.

"Man, it's like this place was just built!" said Jessie.

"There was only one family that lived in it before us, and they only were here for a year before getting stationed somewhere else. They're going through the process of building new houses on this base. Of course, they'd make sure to rebuild the officer housing first," her dad said with a grunt. Even though they lived on the officer side of base housing, her dad was enlisted. They only lived on the other side of the base because of her dad's position.

Sarah opened up the blinds that covered the patio door and pushed them back so she could walk through to the patio. "Oh my! Look out at that view guys!" Although the house wasn't directly on the beach, they were on the sound and had a decent view to it. This was hands down the best house they'd lived in during their adventures with the military.

Jessie ran out of her room with her brand new polka dot bikini, "I'm ready to go to the beach!"

"Give me about twenty minutes and we'll leave," her mom said.

The three of them got ready and headed out the door. Jessie was beyond thrilled to be living at the beach. One of the best things about being a military child, is that you have the opportunity to experience the world at your hand. Jessie was born in Germany and had lived there, along with two other countries, and four different states. Being all of fourteen, that's not too shabby of a travel history. As the family drove up to the parking lot at a nearby pier she shrieked.

"This is going to be so much fun!"

"Calm down, Jessie. It's just the beach," said her little brother, creeped out by her excitement.

"Maybe it's just the beach for you, DJ, but for me, this is the week before my high school career. I understand that you have to go to elementary school at the beach, but I get to go to high school here. It's going to be amazing, I can just feel it."

Their mom was in the front seat gleaming at the joy of her daughter, "Alright you guys, lets go ahead and have some fun on the beach before we have to get home and help dad."

Walking up the boardwalk, they took in the sights that were to be offered by the beach town. Jessie took in every creak of the pier as she walked over each board. At the very end of the pier there was a huge ferris wheel. It was the iconic landmark of many piers. The smell of funnel cakes and hot dogs wafted through the air as they got closer to the ferris wheel.

"Are we going to the beach or the Ferris Wheel?" asked their mom.

"Beach, beach, beach!" shouted DJ.

Jessie squished her cheeks with her palms, "Yeah, sure why not the beach. The ferris wheel will always be there anyways."

The sand felt hot and crunchy underneath her feet. She enjoyed it as it was much more delighting to the senses than the dust of the Earth that Oklahoma had to offer. Once they had found a spot on the beach, they laid out their towels and put on sunscreen. Jessie couldn't help but breathe deeply to inhale all of the saltwater air. It was one of those things where she could taste the air she smelt, and she loved it.

"Man, I'm hungry," she told her mom.

"Why didn't you get something while we were up on the pier?" asked her little brother.

"Leave your sister alone, DJ. Here," said her mom as she rummaged through her purse, "take some money and go grab something to eat."

"Thanks a bunch," said Jessie before she took off towards the pier.

As she stepped off of the steps and onto the pier she could feel the heat blistering up through the wood. "Shit," she said under her breath. She looked up trying to spot the closest place to get something to munch on, when her eyes landed on a hot dog stand. "Perfection!" she gleamed as she hopped over there. It was an odd sight to see a girl hopping from left foot to right foot across the pier, but she did so gracefully.

"One hot dog with ketchup, mustard, and lots and lots of relish please," she said to the man working behind the counter.

"Good choice," said a voice coming from behind her.

She turned around to see the most beautiful guy she had ever laid eyes on. He was at least six foot tall, with abs that could withstand bullets, all while having a dark glossy tan and dark brown hair and blue eyes. "Well, I mean I do like wieners," she said as she took a bite of her hot dog. The cute guy laughed and it hit her what she'd just implied. "Oh, no," she said with a mouth full of processed meat, "I didn't mean." She looked at the hot dog in her hand and back at the gorgeous hunk in front of her.

"I'm Sam. I'd shake your hand, but you've got like, ketchup all over both of them." He grabbed a napkin from a nearby holder and wiped her hands off for her. "There," he said as he placed his hand in hers, "I'm Sam."

"My pleasure," she said, while making sure her jaw didn't drop.

"Whatcha doin, Sam?" asked a bleach blonde barbie that ran up beside him.

"This is....?"

"Jessie," she piped up.

"Yeah, this is Jessie. I was just helping her out with her hot dog."

"I can see that," said the barbie girl as she took Sam's hand in her own. "Well, it's nice to meet you Jessie, but we really have to be going. You know, grown up high school things to do, nothing a middle schooler would know about."

"Actually," Jessie started, "I'm in high school."

"Oh really?" the girl said, making it obvious to look at Jessie's flat chest.

"I haven't seen you around before," said Sam. "Are you new?"

"Yeah I start ninth grade at PCBHS on Monday."

"Ahhhh, so you're really technically an eighth grader. I guess that would explain the lack of boobies. See you 'round two by four!" The evil girl took the hands of the gorgeous hunk as he waved Jessie goodbye.

Jessie made her way back down to where her brother and mom were sitting on the beach. Suddenly she had less of skip in her step. When she plopped down on the towel next to her brother, her mom looked at her from over her sunglasses, "What's wrong?"

"Nothing. Just kind of wondering if this place really is going to be so different after all."

"Why? What happened?"

"It was just, this cute guy was flirting with me, and his barbie doll girlfriend came up out of no where and was just kind of mean."

"What the hell, where is she?"

"It's not that important mom, I mean I'm going to have to start holding my own if I'm going to be going to a high school. Plus, the guy was really nice, it was the girl that wasn't so much."

"Probably just jealousy hun. Girls are like that."

Jessie shrugged and they all laid there at the beach. It was amazing to her how her brother could be at the beach for the fist time in a year, yet still be so glued to his portable video games. She was glad that she didn't have that problem, that she could look out at an open sea and enjoy life for what it was without the constant distraction of technology.

The weekend drifted by without too much excitement. The family had driven by the schools that the children would be going to, so they would get the opportunity to see it for themselves before their first day of school. Down here everything was in a close proximity to one another. Highway 98 split the base in two, her family lived on the sound side with the other officers, while the family's of the enlisted lived on the other side. When you got out on the highway, it would take you wherever your destination was. It wasn't the major highway of a bustling city, but the one of a beach town. You take one turn left and a right and you would be at the high school. Get back on the highway and take a left and you're right there at the beach. One of the most interesting things about the school system there was the times they would go to school. School started at seven a.m., meaning they were to be in class no later than six forty five, but they would get out by one forty five. That was even if they had classes all the way up to seventh period, which many of the juniors and seniors wouldn't even have that many classes any way.

At five thirty her alarm started going off. Jessie slammed the button twice, only to realize that she would have to be at the bus stop in twenty minutes. Leaping out of the bed she ran to her closet and threw on the outfit that she'd picked out the night before to wear for her first day of high school. She had these cute stone washed denim blue jeans and a pink halter top with a pair of flip flops. Living at the beach meant a looser dress code. Running to the bathroom, she slammed into her brother and they both fell to the floor.

"What are you doing up so early?" asked her brother.

"I have to be at the bus stop in ten minutes. Why're you up so early, you have another hour of sleep?"

"I have to pee," DJ said motioning towards the bathroom. "Hence the reason, why I'm on the way to the commode."

"Oh. Well, go use mom and dad's. I have to put at least a little makeup on." She helped her brother get off of the floor and rushed to dab some blush and mascara on. Her skin was still baby soft and clear of acne, so she didn't need to much makeup given her good features.

Just as she was about to run out the door her mom called out to her. "Jessie, you're forgetting something," she said as she held her book-bag high in her hand.

"Oh, jeez. Thanks mom," she said as she kissed her moms cheek.

"Here," said her mom as she handed her a cereal bar and a banana, "You gotta eat something."

"Life saver."

She waited at the bus stop a good ten minutes before the bus arrived. It came to a creaking stop and she walked around to get on board. When she made her way to the top of the bus stairs, she looked up and down the right and left sides of the aisle, searching for a place to sit. She didn't see any open seats, so she started walking to the back of the bus.

When she'd walked halfway through the bus, she heard a voice shout, "Hey Jessie."

Confused, she looked around, unsure of who could possibly know her name on the bus. For a minute she wondered if a kid from another base had just moved here too, but she didn't see any familiar faces. Finally when she had gotten a little bit further back, she could see who was calling her. It was the gorgeous boy from the beach.

"Hey you. Want to share a seat with me?" he asked her.

"You live on base?" asked Jessie as she sat down beside the hunk.

"Yeah," he said chuckling, "I don't live on the sound side though, my dad's enlisted."

"Ahhh, gotcha," Jessie stared at her hands for a minute before looking in another direction. She didn't want to be thought of as a creep for staring at such a good looking guy.

"I'm sorry about my friend the other day," he said, breaking the silence. "She's kind of nutty."

"Oh, she's just your friend?"

"Yeah, just a friend. In fact, she's not even my friend, but one of my buddies girlfriends. She's just territorial and weird."

"Man, I feel bad for your friend, if she's all over every guy like that."

"Some girls are like that I guess."

The two sat in silence until the bus came to a stop at the school. "Well," said Sam, "Hope you have fun. Don't worry too much about making friends. The good one's come to you. The best thing about this high school is everyone's friends with everyone. It doesn't matter what clique you would be in at another school, we all pretty much get along."

"Thanks, I appreciate it," Jessie said as she stepped off of the bus.

As she hopped off of the bus, she stared at the double doors in front of her and took a deep breath in, and a deep breath out. It was her time to shine. She knew that this would be the one town where she would be able to get along with everyone. It was time for a change, time for her to be the fun outgoing girl that she was. Just as she was about to open one of the doors, a kid running off of a bus plowed into her.

"What the hell are you doing just standing there, Fresh-meat?"

"I, I don't know, why weren't you watching where you were going?"

The boy rolled his eyes and nudged his way through the crowd of kids entering the building. Jessie adjusted the strap on her book-bag and started walking through the halls. The tiles on the floor were creme colored, with the random red and black tiles lining the walls. Fluorescent lights lit up the hall, making everything in them look somewhat dimmer than what it really was. She searched for the freshman lockers, and came upon some of the older and bent lockers in the school. When she found her locker she winced at the huge dent in it. Not only was it an old beaten up locker, but it also was a bottom locker. For a girl that was five feet, ten inches tall it would wind up being a pain in the ass.

When she was sitting on the floor unpacking her book-bag and stocking up her locker, she heard a voice come from behind her, "If it isn't mosquito bite." It was the girl from the beach that took off with Sam by the hand.

"Oh, hey," she said, not wanting any trouble.

"Look," the mean girl said as she scanned Jessie up and down, "I don't want to be a bitch to you, so stay away from Sam."

"You're dating his best friend? I don't see what your issue is. Plus, I've only talked to the guy twice."

"Yeah, well he likes you. Saw him on the way in and he mentioned sitting with you on the bus."

"That was like, five seconds ago, though."

"Word travels fast in a small school. Don't worry, I don't want him. He's going through some shit. His brother was just in a major pile up in Connecticut just outside of his college campus and is in critical condition. He doesn't need to take some girl onto his already big enough pile of issues. So be smart, and leave him a lone." The girl stood up and tossed her hair behind her back. Just as she was about to leave she turned back and kneeled down next to Jessie, "Don't make me be a bitch."

When the girl had left Jessie finished putting things away into her locker. She tried to shut the door but because of the big dent in it, it wouldn't close. She tried to shut it from the top and it wouldn't work. Then she tried shutting it from the bottom but it still wouldn't budge.

Finally, she thrusted her whole body, all of ninety pounds, against the locker door and it shut. She slumped down and breathed deeply, "So much for a dramatic change in scenery."

The classes throughout the day went by more smoothly than she thought they would have. Even though she had a run in with the school's diva, it turned out that she was the largest queen bee, and she wouldn't have to worry about too many other people with similar personalities. After all, the girl was just looking out for a friend. For the most part, people at the school were beyond friendly. She may have been just a freshman amongst other freshman, but even at the lunch tables she was able to find friends. When she sat down at a table full of girls she met in her last class, they welcomed her with open arms. They mainly talked about how interesting high school was so far, and that it wasn't nearly as scary as they thought it had been.

Just as she was waist deep in conversation, she made eye contact with Sam who was walking out of the lunch line. He walked over to Jessie, with a chocolate milk in one hand and a ham sandwich in the other. "Hey pretty girl," he said. "I was wondering if you wanted to come hang out after school with me and some buddies."

"Oh, I don't know," she said bashful as she looked between the hunk in front of her and her friends beside her, "I mean, it's the first day of school."

"So? Bring a friend," he said as he shot glances at some of the other girls, "that way you don't have to feel too alone and awkward with a couple of guys. My buddy has a military dad too, so we can take you home afterwords. Text your folks and see if it's OK. with them."

"Ah," Jessie hesitated as she thought about what his blonde friend had told him earlier in the day. She weighted everything that he was going through, and figured if anything she could at least be another shoulder to lean on, "Yeah. Sure. Definitely."

"Cool, I'll meet you in the junior parking lot after seventh period. Sound good?"

"Yeah, sounds great."

When he left all of the other girls started gushing. "Holy crap," Alex, the quirky brunette said, "Do you realize who you were just flirting with?"

"Sam?"

"Yes, Sam. He's a total babe. All of us went to middle school with him and he's not only super gorgeous, but he's a sweety too. You have to go this afternoon."

"I guess, I mean, you want to go with me?" she looked at the girls face and sunk, "You'd have to go with me or I can't go. My parents would freak if I went to hang out alone on the first day of school with a group of guys. It would be different if I had a girlfriend to go along with me."

"Yeah, sure I'll go."

The day drifted on, much more slowly than it had begun. Fortunately for Jessie, the majority of the classes just reviewed what they'd be learning throughout the year. They were introduced to the teachers and their pet peeves, along with what they expected out of their students. It wasn't anything she hadn't dealt with before when she was in middle school, it was just a lot more classes and less space between the classes than she had in middle school.

Finally the seventh period bell rang. At first she had forgotten why she was so ready for the day to be over. Then it hit her that she had plans to hang out with one of the coolest, cutest guys in school and it was only the first day of her being a freshman. Many people would say that the first day is the worst day, but if this was going to be the worst day for her, then she must have some great things coming her way. Just as she was grabbing her books to leave, she remembered that she needed to text her mom to let her know what she was going to be doing.

"OK if I hang out with some friends after school?" she texted her mom.

Her mom texted her back, "How will u get home?"

"Military brats."

"Be home by 5."

Her mom had a great trust for military kids. They were often very sheltered, not seeing too much of the dangers that lurked on the outside of the gates. She thought that if her daughter was going to hang out with some military kids, they couldn't get into too much trouble. They wouldn't be willing to put their parent's jobs on the line just to do something irresponsible.

Jessie dropped by her locker to put some of the text books she didn't need back into their place. While she was sitting on the ground putting her books away, she felt someone come over and tap her shoulder, "How convenient that your locker be a hallway over from my A.P English class."

"Hey, you!" she said excited. "My friend Alex is coming with us, I hope that's OK."

"Of course it is. I think I went to middle school with her, she seems like a fun going type of girl."

"She is. So what exactly are we going to do? Go to the beach or something?"

He extended his hand toward Jessie and when she'd stood up he offered, "I was thinking car surfing."

"I'm not sure I know what you mean," she said puzzled.

"We do it all the time, totally safe. Usually we find an old neighborhood road and you just stand on top of the car as we start driving. We don't go super fast or anything. It's kind of freeing, though. You know?"

"Sounds crazy."

"It's not," said her friend Alex as she walked up to her. "No one ever goes fast enough to get hurt when you go car surfing. As long as they stayed on a neighborhood road, there shouldn't be too much to worry about."

"I guess it could be fun," said Jessie.

"Great!" Sam wrapped his arm around Jessie's shoulder and they all started walking out towards Sam's friends car. It was a little cheap car from the early 90's, but when you're new to driving, parents rarely want to risk buying a brand new car that's going to get dinked to hell and back. They got in the car and drove into a little neighborhood by the beach. When they got there the guys in the front seats looked at the girls in the back seat. "Any takers?" asked Sam.

"I've done it before," said Alex. "I'll go first and show Jessie it's nothing to worry about."

They drove a few roads in the neighborhood at ten miles an hour and nothing happened. When they came to a stop Alex hopped down from the roof of the car. "See," she said to Jessie, "Nothing to worry about."

"We'll take you slow, Jessie. Promise," Sam said smiling.

"Sure, yeah," Jessie said, although she wasn't so sure she should trust them. It wasn't necessarily that she didn't trust Sam, it was more the fact that his friend who she'd never met before was doing the driving. She went through with it anyway.

She climbed on top of the little beat up blue car and held on to the luggage rack. The guys had their windows down so they could hear her if she wanted them to stop. They started out driving slow. Once she was able to stand up they began gaining speed. They were about to stop at the entrance of the subdivision, when they saw a car behind them driving at a quick pace, as there was another car turning in to the subdivision. They would have to take the car out on the open road to avoid being rear ended by the guy.

"What are you guys doing?" Jessie asked them.

"We have to go around the corner to let this guy out, he'll hit us if we don't."

Just then they went around the curb to avoid being rear ended by the guy speeding behind them. As the turned right, the car turned too sharply and to avoid running into the grass, the driver jerked the steering wheel, sending the car plowing head on into the left hand lane. Jessie had managed to kneel down and grab the luggage rack bars again. They began to weave between a few other cars driving head-on. The driver had eyes on the destination, which was a gas station that was only a few yards away. As they were about to pull into the gas station for Jessie to get off of the roof, a car t-boned them. Jessie was thrusted into the air, landing head first onto the pavement. Her neck broke, instantly killing her.

It took nine minutes of car surfing.

Ten

Lane Dawson had his own business that he started from the ground up. He didn't grow up in a wealthy family, so his livelihood rested on his own shoulders. There wasn't any money for college, as far as his parents were concerned. During high school he was insufficient and didn't have good enough grades to gain any form of academic scholarship. When he was eighteen he decided to go out into the world as an entrepreneur. Although there weren't many things he could do, he had studied his mom's beauty rituals. Lane would come up with varying concoctions that were meant to be of supplement for a woman's beauty regimen. Lane would go door to door with his creations and although most would wind up in the trash after a week of peddling through doorsteps, he finally found a product he had made that would interest the likes of an investor.

It was six o'clock in the evening after a long day of walking and trying to sell his product. He had found himself on he doorstep of a beautiful two story home on the lake. After the third knock, the door finally creaked open, "Can I help you?" a gorgeous woman with flowing blonde hair asked.

"Yes, ma'am. I'm Mr. Dawson, and I sell beauty supplies. Given that you are quite the beauty, I was wondering if you might be of interest."

"I'm sorry, dear, but I don't buy anything from pedlars."

Just as she began to close the door Lane became desperate, "Wait! I'll give you two for half the price of one."

The lady turned in her steps and looked at Lane, "What is it that you're selling?"

"It's a dual purpose cream. Not only can it repair the damaged ends of over styled hair, but it can also moisturize the skin, and can fend off wrinkles."

She lifted her eyebrows, "Is that so?"

"Yes ma'am. Like I said, I'll give you two jars for half the price of one."

"How much is that?"

"For you, ten dollars. That's it."

"Just a moment, let me go grab some cash." The lady left to grab some money and returned, "I'll give you twenty for both. I understand the importance of hard workmanship." She looked up at the sky, "Given how brutal the heat's been, I couldn't sleep at night knowing I didn't give you less than twenty." She traded the little jars of beauty for a small side of cash, "Do you have a business card, Mr. Dawson?"

"Yes, I do actually," he said as he riffled through his wallet for his business cared. He handed her the card and waved goodbye.

A full month went by and he had only sold a case of his beauty products. It was time to go back to the drawing board. At least five times a month he would get down to business and create some mastermind plan that would make him millions. When it boiled down to it, he barely would make back enough to cover his costs. Rarely did Lane ever profit from his endeavors. He loaded up his truck with the forty cases of skin and hair products and began driving for the local flea market. Half way there he got a phone call.

"Hello?" he answered his cell phone.

"Is this Mr. Dawson?" asked a man on the other line.

"Yes, may I ask who this is?"

"My name is Carl Henkley. A month ago you came to my door and sold some skin care products to my wife."

"Skin and hair, to be completely accurate."

"Yes, I see. Anyway, my wife loved the products. I could even tell a difference in her skin. Her hair had always looked somewhat fried from being a platinum blonde, and now it's as luscious as any brunette's hair."

"Well, I appreciate the good feedback, but they didn't take off like I expected. I have stock that I could sell you if your wife was interested, but I can't produce products for one customer alone."

"That's exactly what I was thinking, Mr. Dawson."

"So you understand that it's probably best for your wife to find her beauty products elsewhere instead of getting hooked on one product that she would never be able to buy again."

"You're a business man, correct?"

"Yes."

"Then you should start thinking like one. If you had, you would've realized by now that I'm not just interested in buying your products for my wife. Last month you stumbled upon just the right doorstep you need to catapult your beauty line. I'm a CEO of a major department store and am interested in having your products in my stores. Would you be interested?"

"Well, of course, that would be amazing."

"Wonderful, I'll get my secretary on the line and have her set up a meeting within the next two weeks.

Two weeks passed by and the meeting came to a close. They landed on a five year contract, which launched his beauty products out into the universe. He became a successful business man and had all of the money he needed to provide a comfortable lifestyle for himself. Lane would often provide conferences for young entrepreneurs. At one of these conferences he met his future wife. She was a beautiful young twenty something year old with looks that most people would die for. He would have to remind people that not only was she a sight for sore eyes, but she had the brains of Einstein to go along with it. This is what primarily drew him to her. She was gorgeous enough to be the face of his company, but smart enough to tell him when he was embarking up a bad business tree.

"What if," one night he brought up during dinner, "we were to bring other entrepreneurs into our line. Let's say we have some sort of nation-wide contest that would allow beauty masters of all kinds to come pitch us their best products. Then after a panel reviews the products, we find a handful that would be a great addition to the company. It would bring new light onto our company and could gain a following from the youth. They would think that they had some inkling of a chance to make something of themselves."

"That's a wonderful idea, Lane," she said, flipping through a magazine.

"You think so?"

"Oh, of course, especially if your ambitions in life are to help your competition."

"Come on, it could be great."

"Think about it this, dear," she put her magazine down on the table beside her and stared at her husband. "You have a young entrepreneur who busts their ass and is given an easy lift with one of their products. It sits on your line for say, two years, then when people begin to use and love the product they become reliant on it. What happens when those two years are up, and people are still in love with the product? Now they go to the winner of the contest alone, without your name attached to buy their product. You've just given your enemy a ride to the top."

"So we copyright everything." He pulled from the far edges of his mind, "Yes, it'll be set up in a contract so that anyone who ventures into the competition is aware of the fact that if their product does make it to the forefront of the company, then we will gain the rights to produce it and they would render themselves legally bound and unable to produce the product under their own company name."

"Then what they do is they go out and create a product that is exactly the same, with one ingredient different. For all you know it could even be better than the one in our line."

"We'll cover our bases to make sure it doesn't happen."

"Think about this scenario, then. You bring a product on your line that is, eh, so-so. Of course to a panel it looked wonderful, but to the eye of the public, it doesn't go so well. Your name is on it. Yes, the original creator may get some heads to turn, but your reputation would be at stake."

"That's what a panel is for, Mary. Don't you get it?

"I do," she said as she picked up her glass of wine and drifted to the doorway. "What I also understand is I have a husband with far-fetched ideas. It's creative, yes. It will draw people to your name even more, yes. Should you be careful if it is an outlet you'd like to venture out on? Most definitely."

He watched as she waltzed out of the door. Her stilettos tapped down the hallway and past the stairs. It was because of her that he'd been able to maintain a business in a struggling economy. Given the fact that he was one of the prime contenders in the line of natural beauty products, she helped him keep stability. There were often times that would arise where he would have a silly idea that she would toss in the trash. For her to even mention the fact that this one could be profitable meant that it was something that he should embark on.

Lane did his homework on this strategy. He got in touch with his company lawyer who set all of the paperwork into place. All of the fine print was lined with how he would cheat the prospective contender out of a name for themselves. He took his wife's advice on ensuring that it would be impossible for them to use their single product in a line of their own, if they ever were able to sky rocket their career on the back of the contest. The lawyer did draw up a clause that allowed the entrepreneur their small ten percent cut of any profit that would be made off the product they created. Although he was all for the making of money, he couldn't whole heartedly steal someone's product. He could just make sure that they didn't take it anywhere else.

The marketing firm for his beauty line blew the concept out of the waters. Of course, this was open to anyone at any age across America, legally they couldn't step past the foreign boundaries. Commercials were sketched out that would give people the insight they would need to know in order to be apart of the contest. A major selling point for the contest was a magazine advertisement. Even though they would be spending money to market the every day American beauty specialist or concoctionist, they would profit tenfold from the products they'd sell, and of course from the entry fee that the contest demanded. One of their biggest marketing ideas was when they drew up plans that would target each and every beauty guru on social media. Many of these women had concoctions and recipes that they would create in their basement, and post online.

After months of circulating information about the product contest, the board finally had discovered ten products that not only had a great sales pitch, but that actually worked as well as the pitch said it would. These ten products would have to be narrowed down to one. Of course Mary Dawson had a major say in what would be placed under the Dawson Beauty name. She even interviewed the contenders to see how they could act under pressure. She wanted to know their every in and out if she was going to be bringing them into her home. As far as she was concerned, no one would have a place on shelves in her name if she didn't see them as fit.

One of the beauty guru's was a young woman from Colorado. She had beauty, as well as brains, which was one of the most important aspects to the Dawson's. The beauty product that she entered in the contest was a skin plumper and tightener. It could be used on sensitive tissues such as the lips, or under the eyes without irritation, and would allow for juiciness of the lips, and gained plumpness to send away eye bags. The product had even been tested on older women who saw wrinkles becoming less noticeable.

"What inspired your product?" Mary asked her.

"My cousin, actually. I was a few years older than her, but we were still close. Her dad was military and they moved around. She was beautiful. Full of youth, and gorgeous. When she was in town we'd sit around playing makeup. She lived life to the fullest and died a free spirit while car surfing. I had to chase my dreams because she couldn't chase hers."

"That's beautiful. So, Selena, please do tell me about what sets your product apart."

"Well, Mrs. Dawson," she was about to continue when she was cut off.

"Ah, ah. Please, call me Mary."

"Of course. Well, Mary, the product speaks for itself. It's a plumper and tightener which can be used on any of the body, without the slightest sensitivity and it actually works. Women with cellulite can call it gone. Under eye bags, gone. Wrinkles practically vanish."

"A product that works is always a crowd pleaser. Far too often we've come across products that either didn't work at all or only worked slightly. After a few days the body would get used to the product and it wouldn't be as noticeable. You are beyond correct when you say that it works. I've been using it and I love it."

"I'm glad. That's such an honor."

"My husband has a thing for women who test out his possible beauty products. It's somewhat inspiring for him.

When I walked in his life, I became somewhat of a muse for him."

"That's wonderful," Selena said as she stared into the eyes of the beautiful woman in front of her. "What would you say my odds are with my product gaining the spot on your companies beauty line?"

"One hundred percent possible."

"What does that mean?"

"It means I want your product. I like your product, and your product is almost as suitable for our company as you are." Mary turned towards her desk and pulled the contract from her desk, "Of course you've read through the contract, I assume."

"Yes, I have. I do have an issue with the fact that I'd never be able to market the product on my own, though."

Mary laughed under hear breath, and sat on the edge of the table in front of the girl, "We're giving away an opportunity for a bright young beauty expert to launch one of their products under our company name. It's an opportunity of a lifetime. Yes, you may never have the ability to market your product separate from our name, simply because that would make you our competitor, but what are the odds that your product would even make it out of the water without our name on it? Very slim, I assure you."

"I suppose you're right."

"I am right, dear. There's no supposing about it."

The next week they signed Selena to their beauty line. Due to how invested Mrs. Dawson became in the girl, she insisted that along with her product having a permanent home in the company, that she would become a beauty consultant and an addition to the panel that brings new products onto the line. Selena had not only won the contest, but gained the career of a lifetime. Had she turned down the spot on the beauty line because of the fact that it would mean having any rights to her own product, she would've also forfeited the career that she didn't even expect to come attached with it.

A few years after the contest, Selena was sent to New York to talk to beauty columnist from a vanity magazine. For the most part, she had been able to travel a good deal after she was announced the winner of the contest. She went on tours to talk to young women about their beauty products, and even gave women empowerment speeches. For her to have been able to chase her dreams in an age of technology numbness, it was even more so powerful for others to be able to delight in her ventures.

She arrived at her hotel via taxi and was welcomed by the doorman. Selena had never been to such a nice hotel, even when she'd been to other conventions she was always boarded in three star hotels. This one had a revolving door for her to walk through that had gold plating around the windows panels. She was even more astonished when she walked into the lobby of the hotel and saw the beautiful marble floors and the ornate chandeliers dangling from the twenty foot ceilings. Directly in front of her was the check in desk, where men and women who looked neatly put together stood.

"Hello, I'm Selena Richards, and I'm here to check in," she told the clerk.

"Welcome, Miss Richards," the woman said as she typed into her computer. "Hm, I'm sorry but I don't seem to have you listed as having a reservation. Could there be any other name that your reservation would be under?"

"Yes, try my boss's name. I think he reserved it. It's Lane Dawson."

The woman typed away and clicked a button, "Ah!" she said as her face lit up, "Here we are.". She scanned the hotel key and told her the room number. "It's on the tenth floor."

Selena hopped in the elevator and made her way up to her room. Finally she made her way to her hotel room and opened the door to find a gorgeous suite. It had all the fine finishings. Gold plated ceiling tiles, a canopy bed, and a full en-suite kitchen. She moved her way into the bathroom and found a gorgeous claw foot tub and a box of chocolates on the bathroom sink with an envelope next to them. Curious, but confused as to who would've left an envelope, she opened it. "I'll be here two hours after you've arrived" the note said. Unsure of who it could be, but still excited at the mysteriousness, she showered and made herself look good. She recently had a fling with an old friend of hers and had talked in depth about it to Mary. It was possible that since Mary knew she would be in town for the conference, that she'd called up the ex for her. It could definitely be an exciting moment for her, especially in the city of lights.

At ten o'clock there was a knock on her hotel door. She made sure to put her robe on when she walked towards the door. Slowly she opened it to peak out at who was behind it. "Hey there stranger," she let slip before realizing who she was talking to. "Holy crap, Mr. Dawson. I'm so sorry, I was expecting someone."

"I know you were, Selena."

"I'm sorry, I don't quite understand."

He looked into her eyes and said, "Did you like the chocolates?"

"Of course, who doesn't like chocolates," she said before breaking down the fact that he had indeed been the one in her room and left the chocolates, along with the note.

"Mind if I come in?" he asked as he brushed his gorgeous silver fox hair back behind his tanned ear.

"No, I wouldn't want anyone passing by to get the wrong idea."

"Of course not," he said as she led him into her room. "I hope I didn't cross the line."

Selena turned towards him, "Of course you did. You're my boss. Your wife has become a dear friend of mine and helped me get my feet into the beauty industry. I couldn't just betray her like that."

"I must have gotten the wrong idea." He studied her face for a moment, looking for any glimmer in her eye, "I just assumed with how much interest you had in the company, and how often you were making meetings with me to talk over business, that there were some other feelings that were underlying."

"I'm sorry, but your assumptions couldn't be further from the truth. However, by how sly you were about getting chocolates in the room and everything else, I can't help but think that this isn't the first time you've done anything like this."

"Mary and I have had our ups and downs. I love her dearly though, I've never done anything before that would upset our relationship. She's just so stern and never backs down from the wall she places up. This was the first time I've ever attempted anything with an employee, or anyone in general. I'm just a good planner and a good salesperson. I was hoping I could sell you on the offer."

"The offer is off of the table, but I understand Mary's wall. I just assumed that she put it up in front of me because I was an employee at best."

"You're far more than an employee to Mary, but that's just how she is."

"So you know how much I look up to her. Why would you come in and try to start something?"

"Because I saw a light in you that I'd never seen shine. It's a light that I once saw flicker behind Mary's eyes, but only for a second before she turned into the clever mastermind that she has become. You're brilliant. You have beauty and brains, and that of course is what I've always been fatally attracted to."

"Well fortunately, the brains behind this beauty are large enough to know when it's getting late and her boss should be leaving." She gestured her hand out towards the door in an effort to escort him out.

That evening Lane was so embarrassed by his decision to try and have a fling with his employee, that he took a red-eye home that evening. When he arrived home at three in the morning he made his way to the closet to put away his trench coat. He could hear a rustling coming from the kitchen, so he walked over to see his wife, who he assumed had gotten up for a midnight rush to the freezer for ice cream. It wouldn't be the first time she'd been found sitting on the floor in front of the freezer with a large spoon in a quart of chocolate ice cream. He peeked his head around the corner, "Hey there honey," only when he looked around the corner he didn't only find his wife, but their accountant. She was definitely indulging in chocolate, just not the kind he originally thought of.

"Oh Christ!" Mary shouted as she jumped up.

"What the fuck is going on in here!" Lane shouted as he grabbed a knife from out of the utensil drawer. "What is this insanity!?"

"I can explain, Lane, I can explain."

"You little whore," he diverted his attention to the man in the corner about to make a mad dash for his exit, "You little bastard. Get back here." The man took off from the kitchen and Lane continued to chase after him.

The accountant stumbled over the edge of a rug in the living room, and right as he fell, Lane slammed his own body on top of him and began stabbing the man.

Once.

Twice.

"Lane!" shrieked Mary.

Three times.

Four times.

The man struggled beneath the weight of Lane and his butcher knife.

Five times.

Six times.

"Get off of him! Please!"

Seven times.

Eight times.

Nine times.

Ten times.

Lane threw the knife to the side of the room and looked at his wife. "You nasty little whore. You made me do this."

It took ten stabs.

The Boy

Christine Archivald was a strong willed grandmother. As a nurse she took care of military soldiers during the Vietnam War. She had seen the battles and knew that they were surmountable. When those in her life could only see darkness, she would share them the light that she had experienced. If ever anyone mentioned how terrible they had it, she would be the first to tell them the story of someone who had it even worse than they did. Christine Archivald pitied no one, and didn't stand for any mess. Especially when it came to her own children.

One of her children, her only daughter in fact, had grown up being stubborn. It wasn't until she turned sixteen did Christine realize the extent to her hardheadedness.

"Mom, I need to tell you something," said Jeraldine one day after school.

Christine scanned her daughters face. She could read the tone in her voice that something was terribly wrong.

"What is it that you need to tell me, girl?" she asked with squinted eyes.

"I have been seeing someone. He treats me right, and I love him."

"What's the issue?" Right then it hit her like a sack of bricks, "You little whore. You're pregnant aren't you? That's why you've been eating me out of house. You were always pudgy, but I couldn't help but wonder the past few months, when you've been exceptionally fat faced, what the hell was going on with you."

Jeraldine stood there in silence. When she didn't say anything her mom picked up the conversation, "Well what the hell do you want me to do about it? Where's that boy you've been seeing who loves you? You need to be going and telling his damn parents, not me. Get your bags. I don't want any of that bad karma sitting around my house."

"But you're my mom."

"Damn straight I am, girl. But I'm not going to look like a fool in my own house. I've put my foot down. Go!"

Jeraldine packed her bags and left. Her boyfriend ran a prostitution ring, and it was only after she had the baby that she found out about it. She kept her silence and didn't say anything to anyone about it. He was a great boyfriend, after all and he supported his family. How he was able to support his family didn't matter to her, even if it meant the life of another woman. One day after work, she pulled up into the parking lot of her apartment complex where policemen and their cars were surrounding Jeraldine's first floor apartment.

"What the hell is going on?" she asked the cops as she got out of her car.

One walked up to her, "Wouldn't you know," he said just before flipping her on the car nearby and handcuffing her.

"What the hell! Rico! This is all your fault you little asshole," she shouted at her boyfriend as they lead him to the car.

"Screw you, Jeraldine! You knew all about it, and didn't do a damn thing. You were just as much involved as anyone."

Her little boy was sitting in the back seat of her car. He had to watch the whole scene take place. After all but one of the cops left, he walked up to the little boy. "Was that your mommy?"

The little boy nodded.

"I'm going to get you somewhere safe. I promise, OK.?" the officer asked. The little boy shook his head and reached his arms up. The officer lifted him onto his hip and took him to the police station. Eventually the police were able to get in contact with his grandmother. Even though she had never seen the little boy, she still took him home with open arms. He had turned four years old, and she began to regret every minute she let go without seeing her grandson.

Jeraldine and Rico were sentenced to thirty years to life in jail. Jeraldine's mother was given full custody of

Angello. Even though he'd had a rough start in life, Christine made sure that he was going to have the best influences in the years ahead of him. She was so insistent on him not taking the path that his mother and father took, that she was beyond particular about the things she allowed to come through her house. Many would call her strict, she would simply call it protective.

She wouldn't even allow television in the house. Christine believe that over time there had been too many bad influences drifting into television and film. If he ever watched TV it had to be when she was in the room. Even though she liked to keep up with the daily news, she would make sure it was long after Angello went to bed. The news consisted of nothing but negativity and she didn't want it rubbing off on her grandson. Lately watching the news was far more difficult to watch than previous years. In the past year alone there had been plane crashes, shark attacks, a brutal CEO murder, the death and finding of drug over lords. It was too much for her to watch and she definitely didn't want it entering into Angello's mind.

One day she had sent her grandson out in the yard to play. His favorite thing to do on his own was to draw with chalk. Christine wasn't sure if it was something his parents used to do with him that became a line to his parents, or if he was simply like every other six year old and liked to play with chalk. He loved it and he would often run up to his grandmother and beg her to allow him to go play in the yard with chalk. Usually it was stick figures and some sort of scene in nature that he would draw. She would try to talk to him about his pictures but he wouldn't let her know anything about them. If he ever was asked what they were about he'd run inside.

After about an hour of Angello drawing on the sidewalk, Christine went outside. "Hey honey, I made some pecan pie. I know it's your favorite." He kept drawing as if he didn't even hear her speak. "You want to come in and have some? I even have some vanilla ice cream to go along with it. The pie is still warm so the ice cream can get all gooey, like you like."

"Ice cream soup," said the little boy with a grin on his face. He kept drawing, so she went over to his side to see his picture. By the time she got down on his level, she was washed over with a mixture of curiosity and fear from what she saw in the pictures. "Angello, honey. What is this?"

"My drawings?"

"Yes, where did you see these?" She knew she had never let him watch the news, and he'd been living with her for two years, and everything depicted on the sidewalk had happened in the past year. There on the sidewalk were ten different pictures. Each one of them numbered. Each one of them an event that had taken place in real life and were blasted across news stations. Things that she knew she'd never let her grandson see, were being drawn across her sidewalk and detailed so exquisitely that there was no question what they were about.

"I have dreams sometimes. I have to draw my dreams."

About the Author

C. B. Burdette is a multi creative who enjoys any endeavors which cater to the right side of the brain.

https://www.facebook.com/DeathByNumbersNovel
http://cbburdette.blogspot.com/

www.ingramcontent.com/pod-product-compliance
Lightning Source LLC
Chambersburg PA
CBHW032141170626
46808CB00006B/2329